IVAN VLADISLAVIĆ

The Exploded View

archipelago books

Vladislavic

First published by Random House (Pty) Ltd., South Africa, 2004

Archipelago Books
232 Third Street #A111
Brooklyn, NY 11215
www.archipelagobooks.org

Library of Congress Cataloging-in-Publication Data
The Exploded View / Ivan Vladislavić.
LCCN 2016036829 | ISBN 9780914671688 (paperback)

Distributed by Penguin Random House
www.penguinrandomhouse.com

The publication of *The Exploded View* was made possible with support from
Lannan Foundation, the National Endowment for the Arts,
the New York State Council on the Arts, a state agency,
and the New York City Department of Cultural Affairs.

PRINTED IN THE UNITED STATES OF AMERICA

The Exploded View

For Joachim Schönfeldt

VILLA TOSCANA

Villa Toscana lies on a sloping ridge beside the freeway, a little prefabricated Italy in the veld, resting on a firebreak of red earth like a toy town on a picnic blanket. It makes everything around – the corrugated-iron roofs of the old farmhouses on the neighbouring plots, the doddering windmills, the blue-gums – look out of place.

Passing by on the N3, Budlender fancied that he could see Iris at one of the windows in Villa Toscana, watching for him. This was his fifth trip to Tuscany. It turned out to be the last, and so brief it was not even filed away under its own name.

He took the Marlboro Road off-ramp. As he waited at the robot, a vendor thrust a bird into the car, some sort of sock puppet with a stiff comb and a scarlet tongue flickering in its throat. Through the stretchy fabric he saw the man's fist flexing to make the tongue pop. Perhaps it was a snake? He wound up the window and glared at the curio-sellers and their wares, ranged on the verges and traffic islands: a herd of wooden giraffes as tall as men, drums and masks, beaded lapel badges promoting Aids awareness and the national flag, fruitbowls and tie-racks and candelabra made of twisted wire. Arts and crafts. Junk. Every street corner in Johannesburg was turning into a flea market. Informal sector employment (as a percentage of the total): 30 per cent. More?

A man holding a hand-lettered sign asking for money or food came closer between the two lanes of cars, moving from window to window and tapdancing for each driver in turn. The smile on his face flared and faded. He was like a toy you could switch off with a shake of your head. At the bottom of the sign was a message: Please drive carefully.

Budlender tilted his head so that the crack in his windscreen, a sunburst of the kind made by a bullet, centred on the vendor's body and broke him into pieces.

Was he a Nigerian? It was time to learn the signs. A friend of his at the Bank had given him a crash course in ethnography one evening after work, over a pint at the Baron and Farrier on the Old Joburg Road. He and Warren had sat in a booth, speaking softly, as if the topic were shameful, and then laughing raucously when they realized what they were doing. 'Small ears?' 'That's what I said. Little ears, flat against the skull and delicate, like a hamster.' And the point of the exercise? Since he had been made aware of the characteristics – a particular curl to the hair or shade to the skin, the angle of a cheekbone or jawline, the ridge of a lip, the slant of an eye, the size of an ear – it seemed to him that there were Nigerians everywhere. He had started to see Mozambicans too, and Somalis. It was the opposite of the old stereotype: they all looked different to him. Foreigners on every side. Could the aliens have outstripped the indigenes? Was it possible? There were no reliable statistics.

At this point in his career, Budlender had been obliged to combine a passion for statistics, if one could call it that, with a professional interest in immigration. Seconded from the Development Bank by Statistical Services, he was helping to redraft the questionnaires for the national census – those used in the census of 1996, the first non-racial headcount in the country's history, had flummoxed half the population. To make sure that the new versions spoke to everyone, as the brief put it, the drafters had engaged a group of respondents, people with diverse backgrounds (they tried to avoid the old categories of 'race' and 'population group') and in every income bracket (they steered clear, too, of 'rich' and 'poor'). For months now, he had been shuttling between the Documents Committee and his share of the sample, finetuning questions, ferrying revised drafts to and fro. Driving, always driving.

It was the questionnaire that had brought him to Tuscany in the first place.

—

The boundaries of Johannesburg are drifting away, sliding over pristine ridges and valleys, lodging in tenuous places, slipping again. At its edges, where the city fades momentarily into the veld, unimaginable new atmospheres evolve. A strange sensation had come over him when he first drew up at the gates of Villa Toscana, a dreamlike blend of familiarity and displacement.

Villa Toscana.

Everything would be filed later. For now, he was like a man in a film who has lost his memory and returns by chance to a well-loved place. Some significant fact, dropped like a matchstick in the back of his mind, kept sputtering, threatening to ignite.

The architect had given the entrance the medieval treatment. Railway sleepers beneath the wheels of the car made the driveway rumble like a drawbridge, the wooden gates were heavy and dark, and studded with bolts and hinges, there were iron grilles in drystone walls. A security man gazed at him through an embrasure in a fortified guardhouse, and then, satisfied that he posed no immediate threat, stepped out with a clipboard.

Budlender opened his diary on the passenger seat to check the name of the respondent.

'What number is Miss Iris du Plooy?'

'Unit 24.'

There was a pen tied to the clipboard with a length of string, and on the end of it was a little graven image. He twirled the pen to examine it from all sides. A three-headed animal with a shock of orange hair on the crown of its head, six floppy ears and three pink noses. Canine. The noses were erasers.

He filled in the details. Name: Iris du Plooy. These pebbly syllables felt familiar in his mouth, smooth and salty against his palate. Unit: 24. Why did they call them 'units'? Name of company? He wrote Nitpickers. Reason for visit: Nits to pick. A little game he played with the security industry. How outrageous would you have to be before someone called your bluff?

The guard took the clipboard and went around to the back

of the car to check the numberplate. In the rearview mirror, Budlender saw him scratching the side of his head with the many-headed dog and writing laboriously. Perhaps he had noticed the joke. He hitched up his trousers and came back to the window.

'Sorry sir, you've got the wrong number.' As if they were speaking on the telephone.

Damn. The number had been changed to the new provincial system when the car was licensed a few weeks back. Gauteng Province. Without thinking, he had filled in the old number with its concluding T, claiming allegiance to the vanished Transvaal.

'I forgot. I changed to GP plates just last week.'

'It is a wrong number.'

Was he expected to recite the new one? For a moment, he couldn't remember what it was. Then he saw that the guard had already written it down in the column on the right, under the heading 'Incidents'.

Perilous times we're living in, he thought. A little accident, a slip of the pen, can turn into an incident before you know it. Or is it the other way round? Isn't it true that 42 per cent of all road fatalities are pedestrians? That 67 per cent of all household accidents occur in the kitchen? That 83 per cent of all infant mortalities could be prevented if the mothers would follow the basic rules of hygiene?

'You cannot come in.'

The guard seemed almost rueful. Yet there was clearly no point in arguing.

'Could you call Miss du Plooy for me?'

'Yes sir.' He withdrew into the hut.

Repelled at the ramparts. 'Villa Toscana' was printed on a salmon-coloured wall to the left. Below each wrought-iron letter was a streak of rust like dried blood, as if a host of housebreakers had impaled themselves on the name. Would the defenders of this city-state pour down boiling oil if he ventured too close? He got out of the car and leaned against the fender. The fortress-like atmosphere of the place dissipated. The tones and textures were passable, clumpy wooden beams, pastel plaster, flaking artfully, yellow stone. Prince Valiant on the Continent. But the scales were all wrong. Things were either too big or too small. In the door of the guardhouse was a keyhole so enormous he could have put his fist through it, and just below it the brass disc of a conventional and presumably functional Yale lock. He wondered whether the beams jutting from the stone really extended through the walls. They had probably been screwed on afterwards. There was probably mortar in the 'drystone' walls.

Absent-mindedly, he took a calculator out of his pocket, turned it over in his fingers, put it away again.

When Iris du Plooy finally appeared, magically, through an entrance concealed by an angle of the wall, he deduced from her damp hair that she had been in the shower. They spoke briefly. There was not much to discuss, as she had already been informed by mail what was required of her. He handed her the envelope containing the draft questionnaire and left.

Afterwards, when it came to ordering the facts of this experience under the heading *Villa Toscana*, he tried to remember his first impressions of her. They were not features so much as sensations or moods, drifting through him lightly, like steam. Contradictory qualities, softness and angularity, dark italic curls on her temples, the shadowed edge of a wall, her coming and going through the bright bars of sunlight cast down by a pergola that a scrawny bougainvillea had yet to cover. And, as he drove away, the chemical scent of her shampoo.

He had been drawn to a woman before by the way she took hold of the world, the way she lifted things and put them down again, a telephone receiver or a magazine, the way she turned a key in a lock or clicked the nib of a ballpoint in and out. Iris had strange hands, too large and bony to be beautiful, he would have thought, but he was shaken by them. He felt them taking hold of him, brushing his surfaces roughly, picking him up, dropping him.

His second visit to Tuscany was labelled: *Hands*.

He had come to discuss her responses to the census questionnaire. This time the guard let him in at once. To his surprise, the huge wooden gates did not open inwards; instead the gate – for it proved to be in one piece – rumbled away into a slot in the stone, hinges and all, at the press of a button. Signposts of ceramic tile pointed the way to Unit 24. He went along the Via Veneto, he crossed a traffic circle called the Piazza de Siena, he passed the turnoff to Monte Aperto. Unit 17, Unit 21, Unit 24. She was waiting for him outside at the foot of a steep and narrow staircase, and when he had parked the car he followed her up the steps to her apartment. There were arches to either side with signs pointing to Units 23 and 25, there were lanterns made of black iron and blistered yellow glass, and frivolous crowds of poppies in the window boxes. In the glass of the kitchen window he saw a stained-glass motif of a sunflower, and behind it on the sill above the kitchen sink, like an improbably bright and solid echo, another sunflower, which might be real or made of silk or paper, in a blue vase.

She seated him in the lounge and went to make coffee. The rooms in Villa Toscana were small, square and white. The furniture, sparse and spindly though it was, seemed too large. He had the unsettling impression that he had strayed onto a page in a book, one of those picture books that were more interesting to adults than the children they had apparently been written for. He had lost all sense of proportion. He stood up, half expecting that he would have to stoop, and raised his hand above his head, measuring the distance between his outstretched fingertips and the ceiling. At least a metre. Probably, there were municipal regulations. Why did it seem so low?

She brought the coffee in white mugs with blue stripes and sat beside him on the white sofa. He was about to ask her about herself, to begin making conversation, but she said something about getting down to business and shifted her mug to the far corner of the coffee table. He sat forward and rested his elbows on his knees. Opening the questionnaire on the glass table-top and smoothing it flat with her palm, she pushed it towards him. The fingers of her right hand were spread to hold the paper flat. With the middle finger of her left hand – it struck him that she did not use her index finger – she traced along a printed line.

'Mr Budlender…'

'Please call me Les.'

'Les. Most of the first page is fine. Name, address, postal code, it's all quite clear. But this thing about the babies born *before* midnight and people who die *after* midnight?'

Her hands were large and long, almost rawboned, her fingernails broad and flat, and slightly hooked at the ends. They should be painted, he thought. Why doesn't she paint them? He was acutely aware of their bony substance. They reminded him of the seaside, the translucent remains of pallid creatures, as finely moulded as plastic.

'Say I'm sleeping over at my sister's place.'

He focused on the questionnaire. 'If you're coming back the next morning… It says so somewhere. "Members of the household who are absent overnight" blah blah.'

'It's not very clear.'

Her little finger, tilted inward so that its tip did not rest on the paper, seemed to be curling away from the sharp edge of the page.

'This is the crucial bit. "Census records the situation as at midnight between 9 and 10 October as the reference point."'

She had written in the margin in a soft, rounded hand that was at odds with her angular presence. Her knee was a hand's breadth away from his own.

When he left, he noticed the sunflower again through the kitchen door. He imagined a conversation, a bright exchange, in which he made a comment about the sunflower and she invited him to rub one of its petals between thumb and forefinger to prove that it was real, or perhaps false, and then they leaned against the melamine cabinets, chatting easily, laughing.

⸺

He took the N1 towards Pretoria and went off at the Star Stop Egoli. The restaurant, where he had paused several times recently to plan his routes and kill an hour or two, made a surprisingly good cup of coffee. Unlike Iris, most of the people in his sample worked during the day and could only see him after hours. Next on the list was Johnny Constantinou of Olifantsfontein, who would only be home at five.

The Star Stop restaurant straddled the freeway. He found a table at the window, facing south, where he could see the cars rushing towards him. He took the newspaper and the Witwatersrand Map Studio out of his briefcase and opened them on the table-top, but these were just props, a focus for the eye in case some stranger made him self-conscious by sitting opposite. After a glance at the headlines, he put the paper aside. He was in the mood for musing. He shifted his chair and looked straight into the traffic.

It was a perch made for a statistician: he was suspended above a great demographic flow, like a boy on a bridge dangling a hook and line, waiting for the rush hour to thicken. His eye took in the stream of traffic, separated it out into its parts, dwelling on sizes and shapes and shades. Colours washed through the motor vehicle industry, changing with the seasons as surely as the leaves, and the ripples still floated on the surface of this stream. He counted black cars for a minute, converted the sum into an hourly rate. He counted women drivers, did the conversion. Cars for men, cars for women. Rivers of drivers. He stopped counting and let his eye dance across the trends:

roof racks (for luggage, bicycles, kayaks), bull bars, trailers, spoilers, roll bars, bakkies, 4x4s. Entire lifestyles, dissolved in the flow like some troubling additive, like statistical fluoride, became perceptible to his trained eye. Company cars, family cars, new cars, old cars. People were always saying: 'You hardly ever see an old car on the roads in Joburg. Look around you at any intersection, it's nothing but Mercs and BMs. Where do they get the money?' Then again, people were always saying: 'Every second car in Joburg is falling apart, and going like a bat out of hell regardless. It's no wonder the accident rate is sky-high.' Were the roads full of new cars or old cars? There was a lesson in this, which only a statistician seemed capable of learning: as soon as you took account of what people were saying, you lost track of what was actually happening. Just as he lost track now, wilfully, allowing the individual vehicles to dissolve back into a stream of movement, while his thoughts drifted to the last quarter's sales in the motor industry, greenhouse emissions, following-distances, fatalities. Fully nine tenths of the cars involved in rear-end collisions were ignoring the recommended following-distance. Axiomatic: had they been heeding the distance, they would not have had the accident. What is it with people? They treat the rules of the road as suggestions whose limits are there to be tested. They gamble with their lives. Do those arrows painted on the tar make any difference? Little patches of arrows on the road surface and a sign on the verge: *Always see three arrows*. An experiment. Is someone monitoring the results? Sniffing out the trends? How does the accident rate with arrows compare to the accident rate without? If it works, they should be painting them in other places. Of course, if they splash too many of them around, people will grow accustomed to them, just as they grow accustomed to the speed-limit markers, and they'll lose their efficacy. A balance must be struck.

'Michael? Butch. How you doing? Good man good. Listen Mike, that consignment we spoke about?'

Budlender turned his eyes on Butch, a rumpled businessman in shirtsleeves and brightly patterned braces (an idiosyncrasy he might have copied from Larry King), with a sheaf of papers in one hand and a pen in the other, and a cellphone pressed to his ear by a hunched shoulder. He was squeezed between two tables at the window, looking down on the traffic, as if he expected to see Mike passing by any minute. Ready to wave.

Only 35 per cent of South Africans have access to a landline telephone. On the other hand, there are four and a half million cellphones in the country. There are more cellphones than fridges.

Budlender called the waitress to top up his cup and ordered a slice of lemon meringue pie. While he drank the coffee, he glanced through the list of respondents he still had to visit that evening. Three of them after Constantinou: Martha Masemola of The Reeds, which he would have to look up on the map; Eleanor Williams of Vorna Valley Extension 5, ditto; Jimmy Dijkstra of Glen Marais. It would take thirty minutes to get out there. Someone else on the Documents Committee should have done him. Doesn't Stephenson live out that way? Then he pored with rather more interest than was necessary or proper over Iris du Plooy's personal particulars. Her second name was Annabelle. She was twenty-eight years old. She was – in order of preference, presumably – an actress, a model, and a continuity announcer on Channel One. So that was why the name rang a bell. Perhaps he had seen her before?

⁓

It was after ten when Jimmy Dijkstra buzzed him out of the driveway in Glen Marais. Going through the questionnaire with Dijkstra, a civil engineer, had been a production. He proved to be remarkably obstinate, refusing to understand things even when they had been explained to him five times. Is the man stupid? Budlender wondered. Or strong willed? Or merely lonely? He knew the signs of a man living alone. It was not the absence of a feminine touch so much as its delimitation. A bowl of fruit on the table in the hallway, an empty fridge, a sink full of dishes, a pair of pressed trousers over the back of a dining-room chair, running shoes and unopened bills on the carpet in front of the TV. You could tell at a glance, by the whimsical distribution of order and mess, that the woman in this house was the char.

He turned onto the R562 and headed for the freeway. He felt like putting his foot down – there were never speed traps at this time of night – but a minibus was creeping up the rise ahead of him and he could not overtake. He dropped back and flicked on his brights. The taxi was listing so badly it seemed on the point of tipping over. Either the shocks were gone or the load had shifted. On the roof rack were stacks of cardboard boxes, a suitcase, a wheelbarrow, something wrapped in black plastic. A blind with 'Born to Run' printed on it in Gothic lettering had been drawn over the rear window.

Then an indicator began to blink and the taxi slowed again

and wobbled to the left. As Budlender nosed past, a stone shot up off the tar, struck his windscreen and ricocheted away, leaving a crack the size of a man's hand.

Even as he flinched from the impact, even before he saw that the taxi was lurching away down a side road, its headlights illuminating the shacks all around, Budlender realized where he was. A squatter camp had sprung up here in the last year on the open veld between this road and the freeway, directly opposite the new housing scheme. He had no idea what either place was called, but he had seen them from the freeway often enough, under a cloud of smog that drew no distinction between the formal and the informal, and he had passed between the two zones earlier that evening, an arrangement of little RDP houses on one side and a clutter of corrugated-iron and board shacks on the other. Somewhere in this field of mud and rust he had once noticed a bright sign saying Vodacom, where an enterprising builder had used a billboard for the wall of his house. There was only one entrance into the place and that was where the taxi had turned. He could not follow it there. But he braked anyway, with a curse, as if there was something to be done, some case to be made, and pulled over onto the gravel. He would have stopped altogether, but something drifted into range of his headlights: the inner tube from a tractor tyre, a huge black rubber doughnut, and a man reclining in it, with his head thrown back and his arms and legs dangling. He was floating there, in spiky new shoots on a blackened fringe of veld, with his fingers trailing in the ash of burnt grass, like someone bobbing in a swimming pool. The beams seemed to rake him from a shallow sleep, and he raised himself in the buckling rubber, arching his back, thrusting his seal-slick belly into the air, extending his right hand in a gesture of greeting or warning. Budlender took his foot off the brake and rolled onwards in neutral, while the naked man in the tube slid past the window, smiling drowsily, waving, drawn back into the dark wake of the car. Through the rear window, he saw the man bathed for an instant in the lurid red of the tail lights, twisting in the tube and craning his neck as if to meet his eye, and then the tube caved in and he went sprawling. Budlender put the car in gear and accelerated, veering back onto the tar, and the scene in the rear-view mirror was engulfed in a surf of dust.

The man in the tube disturbed him more than the cracked windscreen. He kept seeing him, tumbling silently into the dust. He could hear himself telling the story about the taxi and the naked man to the Documents Committee the next day, and laughing about it, but now he was filled with anxiety.

The crack was a perfect expression of the sound the stone had made when it hit: a jagged star, like two crossed lightning bolts.

When he reached the M1, and reflections of the yellow overhead lights began to crawl repetitively over the bonnet, he saw that the star had five arms. He tried to recall the registration number of the taxi. He should have memorized it. Someone he knew used to do that: make up a mnemonic to preserve the number of any vehicle that struck him as odd, just in case it came in useful later. Was it that friend of his father's? Or was it a character in a book he'd read or some PI on television? Whoever, he liked the idea. Eternal vigilance. He should cultivate that, he should find some odd corner of human life to which eternal vigilance had never been applied, and apply it, just to see what dividends it paid. That numberplate had been in his headlights for a couple of kilometres, it must be lodged somewhere in the circuitry of his memory. BRN… KZN…BGN…RNG. There had been a motto too, in the back window, and a name painted by hand on the panel below. But all of it was gone.

Apart from the news and a bit of sport – cricket, tennis, golf – Budlender did not watch much television. Drama of any kind bored him. As for Channel One, he had never done more than pass through it with a flick of the remote control. It was all music videos and soap operas in languages he did not understand. But now that his census visits were over for a spell (the next round of follow-ups was not due to begin for a fortnight) he spent time in front of the set, nodding off sometimes during the shows, starting awake when the adverts blared out, skipping from channel to channel with the remote as if he was looking for something. So he became acquainted with the continuity announcers and the odd interiors in which they were displayed, generically decorative spaces with crimped and puckered surfaces, draped and folded satin sheens, buckled planes like the insides of chocolate boxes or shop windows, in which they moved stiffly like overdressed mannequins, animated goods. Once, in some public-service advert for abused animals, he thought he saw Iris in dungarees and rubber gloves clutching an oil-soaked penguin, but she came and went in an instant. Why did everything have to happen so quickly? So incompletely? It was nothing but bits and pieces of things. How much of any given hour on the screen was actually explicable to the ordinary person? What proportion of it was composed of objects that were whole, actions that were uninterrupted, sequences that were linked by more than an insistent rhythm? An endless jumble of body parts amid ruins, a gyrating hip, an enigmatic navel, a fossicking hand, a pointing finger, sign language from a secret alphabet, fragments of city streets, images flaring and fading, dissolving, detaching, floating in airtime, dwindling away into nothing. *Simunye, we are one*, the signature tune insisted.

Then, on a Friday evening, as he sat down in front of the set with an instant lasagna from Woolworths on his lap, hot out of the microwave, there she was, trotting out the details of the evening's viewing. She was speaking Afrikaans. Her companion, a young man with muscular arms and a beaded hairdo that made him look like a ritual object, was speaking – what exactly? Zulu? Sotho? He should learn to tell the difference, at least, Budlender considered, even if it was too late for the ins and outs. For all he knew, the fellow might be speaking Igbo. Come to think of it, he did seem to have the characteristic shell-like ears, the 'Igbo ormer', as Warren had put it in his arch way. He and Iris were carrying on a normal conversation, as if they understood one another perfectly. While the one was speaking, the other would gaze out with a look of sympathetic concern, casting sidelong glances of the most natural comprehension in the speaker's direction from time to time, even nodding, or making small exclamations of agreement and support. It was possible, Budlender supposed, that the announcer – if he were not in fact a Nigerian – might understand Afrikaans quite well. But surely she did not understand a word he was saying? It is a fact that no more than 2 per cent of white South Africans speak an African language. Twenty-two per cent of the population speak Zulu as a first language. Nine per cent speak English. Interestingly enough, Afrikaans is more widely spoken than English. He watched Iris's face soften as she turned into profile, harden again as she turned back. Softening, hardening. There was something in her expression that was close to disdain.

The announcements were over. The two of them beamed in unison and disappeared. Budlender flipped idly through the channels again: adverts, infomercials, boxing, news. He dropped the remote and went to fetch the concertina file full of census questionnaires from his study. When he returned to the lounge another programme was just starting. *Homicide: Life on the Street*. What's that supposed to mean? Surely it should be *Death*? He turned the volume down and leafed through the file. Barry, Berman, Constantinou, Dijkstra, Du Plooy. Iris. He extracted her folder from the file. English, Afrikaans, schoolgirl French. Nothing indigenous.

He had the mind of a clerk: each of his encounters with Iris was stored away in his memory like a folder in a filing system. His third visit to Tuscany was labelled: *Duck*. A more evocative title would have been welcome, but he had learned to suppress the urge to reinterpret what presented itself: when a label materialized and stuck to his experience, there was no point in trying to tear it off and replace it with something more elegant.

He had come again, bearing a second draft of the census questionnaire, a clean white version incorporating all the revisions collated by the various fieldworkers. They sat in the lounge as before. He waited for her to sit on one sofa and then he sat on the other, in the L-shaped angle where the armrests touched, with the corner of the coffee table pointing out a safe distance between them. *Always see three arrows*. Genuine leather, he decided, pressing his palm into the cushion next to his thigh. They drank coffee out of the striped mugs while she glanced over the form. What is it about horizontal stripes of a certain proportion that seems *French*? Is it those jerseys worn by sailors? Or are the jerseys themselves repeating a pattern? The sight of her long forefinger crooked through the ear of the mug was disquieting. He wanted to press his lips to her knuckles and taste sea-salt and lemon rind. He took off his glasses and put them down on the coffee table. A touch of vanity. Without the glasses, she seemed softer, less abrasive.

'This all looks fine to me now.'

'No problems? I'd be happy to work through them with you. That's what I'm here for.'

'No, it looks fine.'

He put on his glasses again and brought her back into sharp focus. She was looking at him with an expression that seemed intensely, almost angrily intent. Furious. She was furiously aware. There was a slight cast in one of her eyes. How odd that he had not noticed it before. Perhaps that was what gave her this look of angry penetration? Iris. Her name was derived from a flower, he assumed, but it evoked the sea-green of her eyes, fixed upon him, upon a point inside him, as if what might be taken for a defect was in fact some special power of insight that allowed her to see through him.

This gaze redefined him. He had the urge to unsettle her, to turn the tables.

'You must remember that this new version of the questionnaire contains the other respondents' input as well as your own. People have very different responses. Something that's clear to me might seem totally obscure to you. You'll have to look at it carefully.'

'I haven't got a lot of time today.'

'You did agree to do this.' He almost added, 'And you are getting paid for it.'

'I've got to be in the studio at half past five.'

'It won't take long. Let's just go through it together quickly. Let's see. This paragraph here, p-11. "Sub-place." Do you understand that?'

'Sub-place?'

'It says here: Main place (city, town, tribal area, administrative area) and Sub-place (suburb, ward, village, farm, informal settlement). Do you understand that?'

'I think so.'

'How about Villa Toscana? In which column would you put that?'

The document began to crumble. At first, she was flustered. Later her furious focus returned, and she seemed to enjoy picking away at every apparent certitude. Five o'clock came and went. He made notes on the copy in red ink. He kept wanting to kiss the side of her head or slide his ink-stained fingers under her skirt. Through it all, he had the sense that he was performing. Not just behaving badly but *acting* badly.

'Could I use the bathroom?'

She pointed to a landing on the stairs, which must lead to the bedroom on the upper storey.

He had anticipated a clean white space, where he would wet his fingertips and wipe the corners of his eyes, and look at himself in the mirror, from one side and then the other, like a man in a movie, composing himself. Instead, there was laundry everywhere, pegged to lines over the bath, draped over the towel rail and the sides of the washbasin. She was inclined to conceal herself, he had noticed, beneath loose-fitting blouses and full skirts. Her underwear evoked her naked body, but he could not imagine it precisely, all he saw was bits and pieces of other women, the thighs of his last lover, breasts out of magazines, hips and shoulders that were ambiguously, softly angled, like her face. He touched the collar of a shirt. Every impulse he had to press something to his face, to breathe something in – her towel must hold the memory of her shampoo in every fibre – felt ridiculous and false, like something he had seen someone else do and now felt obliged to imitate. He thought of panty raids in college residences, rock star fantasies, peepshow paraphernalia. He sat on the edge of the bath. There was a yellow sponge in the shape of a duck roosting on the soap dish. He picked it up and found that it was sodden. He squeezed it so that the water ran out between his fingers. Then he caught sight of his face in the mirror over the basin, looking out from behind a skyline of bottles and jars, like a man in a wanted poster. He put the duck back on its nest, flushed the toilet guiltily and returned to the lounge.

Soon he said he had to leave. He was grateful to her for making the time to go through the questionnaire so thoroughly. He would be back in a week with the third revised draft. Did Wednesdays suit her?

In his rush to get out of Tuscany, he took a wrong turn and got lost. At first, he was irritated. Not just with himself for his carelessness, but with the whole ridiculous lifestyle that surrounded him, with its repetitions, its mass-produced effects, its formulaic individuality. But then this very shallowness began to exert a pacifying effect on him. Gazing out at the pink and yellow facades, rumbling over the cobbled speed bumps that kept the car down to a walking pace, he grew calmer. He felt the tension leaving his body, draining out into the afternoon, almost visible, like some dark strand on the pastel air. He rolled the window down and dangled his arm in the breeze, trailing his stress behind him like a purple ribbon. On a slope down into the valley, where the distant freeway hummed, he put the car in neutral and coasted, betting on himself to get over the next speed bump.

He went round in the complex for three quarters of an hour. Once, a security guard on a bicycle stared at him suspiciously, but he gave him a cheerful wave that set his mind at ease. Twice, he passed the ceramic signposts pointing the way to Unit 24. Twilight sifted down, and the lights started coming on in the windows. When he saw the sign pointing to Unit 24 for the third time, he turned into Viale Pretoriano and coasted past her home. The lights were on in the kitchen now, causing the yellow sunflower to bloom again with its face turned to the world, even as the sun went down over the rooftops. The traffic increased. People coming home from work, cheerful Tuscans, rudely healthy and well dressed, banging the doors of their cars, fetching briefcases and grocery packets from their boots, pressing the remote control devices that switched on the alarms of their obedient recreational vehicles.

In a distant corner of the complex, on the loop of road containing Units 71 to 84, he came to a map on a board and used it to find his way back to the gates.

～

Falling in love. Falling? He had plunged off the edge of himself. Night after night, when he lay down to sleep, he repeated the false step and plummeted. Just as he was dropping off, he would start up awake, with his arms flung out and his fingers hooked into the duvet, like a man clutching at clouds.

He calculated, in these early hours, that he had been 'in love' no more than half a dozen times in his thirty-seven years, including a teenage infatuation that had never progressed beyond a fever of hopelessly embarrassed desire. What proportion did this represent of all the women in his life, including those he had slept with, with whom he might have fallen in love? It was a pointless question – the terms were too vague, the variables too numerous – and yet it had, nonetheless, a perfectly adequate answer. A negligible proportion.

Negligible. The unhappiest of statistical terms.

Iris. Why did he find her flaws so appealing? On her left cheek was a tiny scar which the make-up department could not conceal. It was shaped like a boot and it reminded him of Italy. Everything about her made him think of Italy and the ocean. It was Tuscany, it was the sadly unconvincing atmosphere of Tuscany in which she had chosen to live. It brushed off on everything like cheap paint. When he asked her out to dinner, which he had resolved to do, he would suggest La Rusticana. He was sure she loved Italian food. Seafood.

Then he lay awake, clutching fistfuls of down into cumulus, suspended between the floor and the ceiling like a human sacrifice. The mattress felt to him like the soft edge of a bar graph. It rose and fell like liquid in a tube, and he floated on its yielding surface, rising and falling with it, growing more or less fortunate as his lifespan expanded and contracted, reacting to every variable – the levels of pollutants in the atmosphere, the radiation from the microwave, the radiation from the eight cellphone calls he had made that day, the possibilities for accidents raised by the three hundred kilometres he would travel the next day to see Constantinou, Masemola and distant Dijkstra, the limitations on injuries produced by the wearing of a seat belt and the provision of airbags in the doors of the Elantra, the risk of heart disease, the hedging of that risk by the eating of polyunsaturated margarine, by walking up stairs even when there were lifts, by going to the gym, by eating red meat no more than twice a week – his spirits rising and falling with all these considerations, while in his mind the thought came and went that he had just 28 per cent of his life left to live, if he was fortunate enough to be an average man.

The Perfumed City.

They had gone through the third draft of the revised questionnaire, lingering over the meaning of 'population group' – the question about race had been the most difficult one of all to formulate; and the definition of a household head – 'The head or acting head of the household is the main decision-maker.' He was in a daze, watching her hands on the paper, memorizing the shapes of her fingers, the lines on her knuckles. The coffee cups, which had looked so French to him at first, had been newly glazed with Italian. The dinner date. How would he leap to that topic across a river of sunlight? They had not exchanged a personal word. He should make small talk, introduce a few little touches about himself, create a profile. Perhaps Occupation (p-19c) and Hours worked (p-19d) would open a door? He could make a comment about the difficulties of working at night – they were in the same boat – and suggest lunch. This Sunday?

A cellphone rang. The theme from *Mission Impossible*.

'Do you mind if I take this?' She had traced the phone to an occasional table. 'I'll just be a minute.' Withdrawing into the next room, closing the door behind her.

Is there a man in this household? he wondered. Is the absence of men as easy to detect as the absence of women? To a man. To a decision-maker.

He went to the window. In the cobbled courtyard below, he saw a rotary washing line, a gas braai, some bags of lawn clippings. No sign of a lawn mower. No sign of a lawn either. Perhaps it was just the grass-green of the plastic bags that had given him the idea. The people next door had a plunge pool that took up their entire yard. He gazed over rooftops of terracotta tile to the boundary wall laced with electric fencing, and then the sweep of veld beyond it and the freeway. You should be able to hear the traffic from here, but not a whisper. Double glazing. He turned back into the room and stood in front of the dresser. There were a dozen CDs on a rack and he ran his fingers down the spines. Sade, the soundtrack from *Cats*, Dance Krazy Volumes 1 and 2, Cole Porter. Framed photographs standing on the dresser. This one must have been taken at work, an office outing, the Christmas lunch. And on the wall a composite family portrait, a dozen snapshots framed in little oval and rectangular windows. Mom, Dad, sister. She spoke about staying over at her sister's place. Who's this? He looks very familiar. Undoubtedly famous for something, can't remember what. Is he an actor? Or is he that fellow who got shot in a hijacking – the one they said would never walk again, who surprised them all by waltzing at someone or other's wedding? He passed along the wall, gazing at the photographs like a gallery visitor, until he came to the foot of the stairs.

He went up the short flight to the bathroom and locked the door behind him.

No washing over the bath this time. He lifted the lid of the wicker laundry bin and saw a plastic bag full of clothes pegs in the bottom. Charlady must have come yesterday. No, if that was the case, yesterday's clothing would be in the bin. This morning then. A towelling dressing-gown on a hook behind the door. Just one bottle of shampoo on the rack in the shower. He flipped up the top and sniffed it, but it was not the scent she carried about with her.

He turned to the counter beside the washbasin. This was what had drawn him back here, he realized. He had never seen such a mass of cosmetics. An immense feminine clutter of bottles, jars and tubes, doubled in the mirror behind. Sample sachets of moisturizer and eye make-up remover, cotton-wool balls in marshmallow colours, tubes of mascara, brushes and wands. Tortoiseshell clips, stretchy hair bands with scribbles of black hair caught in them, combs, tongs. A pink plastic razor, the flimsy kind of thing a woman would use. Emery boards, nail varnish, acetone.

A dim memory from his childhood came back, like a stranger into a shadowed doorway, and went away again without speaking: *baking* with the girl next door, with Melanie, mixing up a concoction from the kitchen cupboards while her mother was at work, a bit of everything, cornflour, salt, sugar, cinnamon, cochineal, olive oil, yeast, making a putrid batter that got more and more revolting with every ingredient they added, until they had to pour it from the mixing bowl into a hole in the back garden.

On the shelf above the basin was a little Manhattan of perfume bottles. There were bottles of every shape and size, crystal and smoked, corseted and shoulder-padded, pinched into feminine shapes or squarely masculine. He opened a tapering glass pyramid with a shiny top. Too sweet. Smelt of overripe oranges. The slim tower was Dolce & Gabbana.

He unscrewed the bright-red cap. Also unfamiliar. Why does she have all these things if she doesn't use them? Dozens of miniatures, which he supposed were samples. Presumably she was always receiving such things as gifts in her line of work. *Romance.* He ran his fingers over the glass with its Beardsley curves and bevels. He was about to unscrew the cap when there were footsteps on the stairs. He put the bottle back in its place and flushed the toilet. The footsteps receded sharply on the white tiles, were absorbed briefly into Chinese silk in the hallway, and tapped again more quietly into the lounge.

He could not leave, although he wanted to.

He went on with the survey. The next sample stood alone on the end of the shelf, a little round red box with a fez tassel dangling from its gold-rimmed lid, and inside it a bottle shaped like a skittle made of fluted glass, with a round stopper, just like a miniature brandy decanter, and another silky tassel tied around its neck. *Valentino.* He pulled out the stopper and the liquid splashed over his hands. In an instant this smell was everywhere, there was no need to breathe it into his lungs off his fingertips, it had poured into the air around him, fruity, over-elaborate, suffocating. He put the bottle away. The dots on the taps were in the Italian colours, as always. He opened them and let them run until the one on the left began to get warm, and then he soaped his hands and rinsed them. But the scent lingered. If anything it seemed to intensify, as if he had left the stopper off the bottle.

'Are you all right?'

He hadn't heard her coming back. Or had he been mistaken about the footsteps? Perhaps she had been listening outside the door all this time. Not that there was anything to overhear. Could she smell the scent seeping out through the cracks?

'Mr Budlender?' She would not call him Les. 'Is there a problem?'

'I'm fine. I'll be out in a minute.'

Probably thought he was trying to steal something. What would she make of him? Did it matter? He washed his hands again, stuffed them in his pockets and went back to the lounge. She was standing behind the sofa with one arm across her chest, the cellphone raised halfway to her head.

When they said goodbye, she held her smile too long. He recognized the look: it was the one the continuity announcers got on their faces when the camera failed to cut away at the end of a segment.

In the blue vase on the window sill there were tulips, shame-faced and round-shouldered. The sunflower must have been real after all.

On the way out to Jimmy Dijkstra's a little later, he realized that there could not be a man in Iris du Plooy's life, if she was being honest on her questionnaire. But why should she be? It was just an exercise, after all. She might have made up a new persona for herself. She could be anyone she chose.

Dijkstra would keep, he decided, and headed for home. All the way he kept an eye on the crack, expecting it to fork out through the glass.

⁓

She was on television again that evening. Alone, in a blue dress that left her shoulders bare and showed him, for the first time, the fullness of her breasts. A microphone clung to the fabric like a scarab. Earlier that day, under Tuscan skies, her skin had looked darkly tanned, but now she seemed unnaturally pale. An effect of the light.

Tonight she was speaking English. Her Afrikaans accent lay on the words like dust from a country road. It charmed him, as always, but the script she had to parrot was so banal he could not listen. It would be better in silence. He would be free to watch the planes of her face, to consider the way she was assembled, to extrapolate from the curves of her breasts to her belly, her thighs.

He reached for the remote control, and in that instant she was gone and an American music programme began. The Top Forty. He turned the volume down anyway and slumped on the sofa, with a tumbler of whisky resting on his stomach, watching the silent play of images on the screen. A man in an office, at the window, against the glass, looking out on a skyline, New York perhaps, although he could not see the landmarks. A man in white in a black space. The man moved from one empty room to another, running his image like a soft cloth over reflective surfaces, over the glass and steel housings of devices, unidentifiable racks of equipment, hi-tech machines that might be made for processing information or meat, he kept walking through the empty rooms, which made up an office or an apartment. The camera followed him from above, a small white ideogram crawling across a shiny black floor. Images on the walls, things in frames, photographs or windows into other rooms where colour was permissible. The camera went outside into the night. It was warm out there, you could feel the air rising up from the pavements below, with something sugary in it that set your teeth on edge. New York, he was sure of it now. You felt the heat around the camera by the longing way it looked through the windows of the apartment or the office into the spaces beyond, which were undoubtedly cool, into the cool spaces you had already walked through, where the man in white was still walking now, with the soles of his feet and the black tiles whispering together, appearing in one window after another, like a sequence of photographs.

He must have dozed off, because now credits were speeding upwards on the screen. His eye picked out a name here and there – best boys and grips, standby painters and casting agents, a Waiter in Restaurant, an Old Woman in Laundry – held these words on the surface of memory for a moment, let them flit back into forgetfulness. Why did these particular names attract his attention? What was the physiology of it, the sociology? The dance of the eye across the information.

Iris reappeared. The satin drapes in the background had changed colour and were now crimson instead of blue. Perhaps they were not made of satin at all but of mere light, lamps trained on a wall or a screen, distressed surfaces. Or they might be projections like the maps and charts behind the weatherman, combinations of colours and textures chosen off a menu with a click of the mouse. He had no idea. Just as he had no idea, when he watched the news, whether the pillars were really made of marble or the desktops of granite. Common sense told him they could not be real. But how could he be sure? Perhaps all the people he saw on television, the newsreaders, the pop singers, the talk-show hosts and the continuity announcers, were suspended in empty space, waiting for an appropriate world to embrace them.

He reached for the remote but it had slipped down between the cushions, and so he lay back and watched Iris in silence.

He became aware of a strange agitation in her body. Her hands were out of sight, severed at the wrists by the bottom of the screen, but he could tell that they were moving. Perhaps she was fiddling with a pen? Her shoulders were dipping and twitching too, her upper arms quivering. You would have thought she was sobbing, although her face suggested the opposite. The smile never left her lips for a moment, she spoke through it, like an actor speaking through a mask. He scrabbled again for the remote, and as his fingers closed on it, she glanced down into the corner of the screen, as if the movement of his hand had caught her attention, gazed out intently with the smile fixed on her face, and disappeared.

How strange it is, he thought, that the continuity people, that they especially, should lead such discontinuous lives.

Budlender's fifth and last trip to Tuscany had no professional purpose to begin with – a dinner invitation could scarcely be considered professional – and predictably came to nothing.

He had invented an excuse to see her. He phoned. Would she be prepared to check the final revision of the questionnaire? He found her comments particularly valuable.

'I'm really busy. Can you fax it?'

But he insisted on bringing it over in person.

In the event, the guard would not let him through the gate. Mr Budlender? Miss Du Plooy was out. She had left instructions that the package should be entrusted to him. Mister – for a second Budlender heard 'Master' – could see for himself, she had written it down. The guard came out of the hut and shoved the clipboard through the window. As he read the message in her familiar hand, he noticed that the guard had acquired a stick with a carved handle: a creature with many heads, an enormous version of the idol on the end of his pen, glowering in every direction.

Villa Toscana, seen from the N3 as he drove back to the office, was less convincing than ever. You might have thought it was made of cardboard and paper, as if the building contractor had taken the architect's model too literally. The stand of bluegums on the plot next door looked like shabby old men, irritable and disapproving.

A few days later, she returned the questionnaire by post. There was a note attached, on a yellow sticker, to say that it was perfect just as it was and she now considered her part in the project at an end. As he smoothed the form out on his desk, he imagined her folding it in thirds, flattening each crease between the nails of her thumb and middle finger, with her little finger crooked in the air.

One night not long afterwards, he dreamt that he was walking in a foreign city, down avenues lined with skyscrapers. The buildings were like bars in a gigantic graph, but they were also perfume bottles, glass towers filled with liquids coloured like honey and brandy. The air was so thickly scented he could hardly breathe. He began to run, over tiles of tortoiseshell and pewter, gathering momentum painfully, step by step, until his feet detached from the earth and he found himself falling, horizontally, through the perfumed streets.

AFRITUDE SAUCE

A long day dusted with talcum powder, chilli powder, paprika. Egan shut the door on it and breathed the recycled air of his hotel room gratefully. While he was out to dinner, the chambermaid had come in to draw the curtains, switch on the bedside light and turn back the covers. On the freshly plumped pillow a chocolate in golden foil rested like a coronet.

How much importance should he attach to these details? They were hardly personal touches – although management would want to think of them that way – they were merely steps in a routine, the writing paper, the matchbook opened like an easel in the ashtray, the ragged carnation in a vase on the dresser. Special effects, produced and directed by the hospitality industry. Yet he felt warm inside, he felt welcomed, despite himself. The booze at Bra Zama's African Eatery had softened him up. Not to mention an afternoon in Hani View. And then, admittedly, it was a better hotel than he was accustomed to. On his Joburg trips, he usually ended up in some sub-economic chain near the airport, a Formula One or a City Lodge, bland places in which software salesmen and retail buyers were propped like cardboard cut-outs advertising beer. Economizing. Egan, Gessing and Malan doing their bit for reconstruction.

He switched on the TV and sat on the end of the bed. When he bent to unlace his shoes, he noticed that he had dribbled gravy down the leg of his trousers, all the way from knee to turnup. The trickle-down effect. Afritude Sauce. What would his dinner companions think? But would they have noticed? Not bloody likely. Half-cut, all of them, like himself. Foolishly, he began to count the yellow stains, moving his forefinger from one island to another, lost count, started again. He leaned closer. Babyshit yellow. No wonder he'd started out thinking the stuff was inedible. Although it had turned out to be delicious. Was it *indelible*?

He emptied his pockets onto the dresser and stepped out of his pants. What should he use on the stains? Something that wouldn't make them set. Janine would know, with her files full of 'household hints'. She was a stain specialist too, everything from getting red wine out of the carpet to getting bubblegum out of the kids' hair. But it was too late to phone home now, he would have to improvise.

In the bathroom, he tore the corner off a sachet of shampoo between his teeth, squeezed a blob of orange gel onto the stain and worked it into a lather, rinsed it out under the tap. Apparently the Afritude Sauce did not come out as easily as it went down. There was something yellow in it. Turmeric. What had the menu called it? *Borrie*.

He filled the basin and squashed the pants into the water. The air-filled fabric popped out like flesh between his fingers, surprisingly resistant, almost muscular. It was like drowning an animal. He lathered one of the little cakes of soap between his palms until the surface of the water was thick with foam. The pants could soak overnight.

Then he flopped down on the bed again and thumbed the remote. CNN, SABC 3, Channel 1. *Simunye, we are one*. There was an 'adult' channel, but you had to pay for it. Would it show up on the credit card? Or would they employ the financial equivalent of the plain brown wrapper? *Raging Bull* was on the in-house movie channel at 10:45. That might be worth staying up for. Time for a shower before the show, and lights out by 1:00.

The shower attachment kept sliding down on its chrome bar. Made for a midget. In the end, he left it at shoulder height. The head – what do you call it? the rose – wouldn't adjust either. He twiddled the switch, but the water kept thudding out in spurts, too hot or too cold, and eventually he turned his back on it, let it pummel at his shoulders, rinsing away the tension, scalding him a little, while his mind walked the stations of the day.

Milton Mazibuko had been waiting for him outside the municipal offices in Kempton Park that morning. To tell the truth, he'd been expecting Bhengu, the town clerk, but the great man was otherwise occupied. Mazibuko was the council official in charge of housing subsidies and deed registration on RDP projects like Hani View. He was a small round man in the cruel grip of fashion – thickly treaded shoes that made him look like a wind-up toy, a Nehru collar as tight as a tourniquet, a watchstrap like a manacle on his wrist. He shook hands with Egan through the window of the hired car and then squeezed into the passenger seat.

Although Egan knew every square centimetre of Hani View on the plans, he had never set foot on the site. Mazibuko gave him directions to the R562.

They small-talked their way through the morning rush hour.

'How are things in Hani View?'

'No, everything is going good.' Mazibuko crossed his short legs in the narrow space in front of him and rested his knee against the dashboard. 'Rubicon finished another fifteen houses last month. The people have moved in already. We had to put them in quick-quick before there was even glass in the windows, so that the squatters didn't get there first.'

'So you're on schedule?'

'Well, let's say we're not further behind schedule than is strictly necessary.'

'Any more blackouts?'

'No, we sorted that out. It was a mix-up at the substation. The big problem is still with the toilets, I'm afraid. Half the houses don't have water. I mean, they've got pipes, but the people can't pay, and so we have to cut them off. Then they complain that the toilets don't work.'

'That's why we call it water-borne sewage, folks.'

'Some of them say they don't want a stinking toilet in the house any more.'

'A little bit late in the day to change their minds, don't you think?'

'Very. Now, when they see the size of the water bill, they'd rather have a long drop in the yard. But when we offered them pit latrines to begin with, they were all up in arms. You remember the story: "I don't want a hole in the ground, like a dog, I want a throne at the end of the passage."'

'It's the same everywhere.' If Janine could hear me now, he thought, this petulant tone. 'People are never satisfied.'

'Exactly. "I want to shit in style and pull the chain, like the madam."'

Mazibuko gave another chubby laugh, and Egan forced himself to join in. This kind of racial humour, or was it interracial humour, made him uncomfortable. He was never sure whether it was for his benefit or at his expense. When a black associate called him 'baas', he got the joke, give or take. But when the same associate called *himself* 'boy' or 'bushie', Egan was never sure what was really going on.

He saw the inevitable morning that lay ahead. Air-borne sewage. He would have to take a whole lot of crap. It was one of his jokes: in this line of work, he would say, you have to take a lot of crap from the customer. You could call yourself a sanitary engineer, if you liked, you could even be a sanitary engineering consultant. Sooner or later, everyone figured it out: you were in the shit business.

From a distance, he'd thought there was a veldfire blowing smoke across the road or something burning in the shack settlement he'd already noticed on the left, a patchwork place of the kind that still made him uneasy, no matter how often he came across it. But as they approached the crossroads, he saw that it was dust from the gravel that traffic between Hani View, on one side of the road, and its informal satellite, on the other, had scuffed over the tar. Both areas were fenced off from the main road and there was just a single dirt track leading off to either side.

The history of the area was complicated. The formal housing project had been an initiative of the Kempton Park council, designed to take the overflow from Tembisa. Two thousand houses in the usual unbending rows, a school, a community hall, a clinic. Louis Bhengu had scarcely turned the soil for the foundations of the hall – an embarrassing moment: the ground was so hard he could not drive the blade of the spade into it, despite repeated blows from the heel of his Bally slip-on – when an informal settlement sprang up on the opposite side of the road. Sprang up overnight, quite literally. The squatters had been dumped there by the Midrand council, on a tract of waste land acquired from the province. Although Hani View Extension 1, as it soon became known, was nominally under the jurisdiction of Midrand, its proximity to the housing project on the other side of the municipal boundary effectively connected it to the neighbouring council. The people from the shacks sent their kids to school in Hani View, they brought their broken bones and whooping coughs to the Hani View clinic, they drew their water there and carried it back across the road in tins. If these people were *ours* it would be different, ran one editorial in the *Express*, but they've been left on our doorstep.

Egan always found it strange to set foot for the first time in a place he knew from the plans. It was like folding out of two dimensions into three. You could almost hear the creases popping as you broke through the barrier. Sometimes it was disenchanting. You had convinced yourself, looking at the neatly inked blocks on the paper, at the street names, the community facilities, the cookie-cutter trees, that the place was rather pleasant. You imagined gardens, shady avenues and parks. And then you got there and found rows of impossibly small houses, not a leaf in sight, dust everywhere, shadowless walls, and the immense blue well of the sky, which reduced the earth to sediment. At other times, the contrast between the flat world of the plan and the angular world of the township galvanized him. It was a beginning, wasn't it? You couldn't expect everything to change overnight. That was half the problem – it was like the pop song – people wanted it all, wanted it now, for free.

They turned into Hani View. The main road had been graded recently and spread with gravel, which rattled against the underside of the car. The whitewashed pegs along the edge of the roadway, where a ridge of sand had been piled up by the graders, suggested that they would be tarring soon. It would make a difference, it would damp down these shifting sands, fix things in place. He turned left into a side street, left again, following the thrusts of Mazibuko's manacled hand, passed between rows of identical houses, and drew up on the verge at the end of the block.

The manhole cover, set in a pad of new cement as pale as a mushroom jutting out in the middle of the dusty street, was oddly reassuring. It suggested that something meaningful was going on below the surface: pipes had been laid, a lasting claim had been embedded in the earth, and would not be rooted out too easily. By contrast, the freshly painted houses on all sides rested lightly on their bases, as if they had been set down there just a moment ago and could be brushed aside with the back of your hand. The electricity poles smelt of creosote. Everywhere the earth had been raked until it was raw. In time, as people lived here, and covered the soil with tar and stone and brick, the human presence would thicken. Permanence grew like a crust. Every layer added depth. In an established city, where every square metre had been patched, paved and repaved, an open ditch could throb like a wound. Workers clustered around a manhole, surrounded by striped barriers under a makeshift awning of green canvas, would remind him of nothing so much as surgeons in the operating theatre, gazing through pegged back skin at the exposed nerve.

'Do you think it is too high?' Mazibuko asked, gesturing towards the cover.

'Seems okay to me. Once the road's been surfaced it should be level.'

'Last week, a taxi driver ripped the sump out of his Mazda on one of these in 10th Street. The people have been complaining.'

That's hardly my fault, Egan wanted to say. It's your responsibility to get the roads paved. Why doesn't the council just get on with it? But he bit his tongue.

They got out of the car and walked over to the manhole. Mazibuko tapped it with the toe of his shoe as if he was trying to make his mark on it, just like L. Z. Mkhonto, who had scored his name and last month's date in the cement when it was wet. It was all too new for its own good, it needed time to settle and mature.

They walked back to the car. Egan took out the development plan lying on the back seat and unrolled it on the bonnet. Mazibuko pinned the corners with his pudgy fists and they pored over the plan together, tracing the branching out of water and sewage reticulation, lighting grids, boundary fences. Egan marked the progress off with a felt-tip pen as they spoke. They had stopped in a good spot, quite by chance, he thought, on a rise at the edge of the built-up area, beyond which the open land sloped gently down to the vlei. He could see exactly where they had got to with the roads and the electrification.

'Those are the new houses down there, the ones I was telling you about earlier.'

Egan put blue crosses through the relevant blocks on his

plan. He dotted in the latest telephone poles and the new roads laid out beside the vlei. There would be trouble there, you could see it from a mile away, they were building too close to the floodline. In the distance, he could see the excavation for the last of the sewage connections, with the pipes laid out on the edges of the trenches.

When they had been speaking for a while, he became aware that a small crowd was gathering. The usual collection of women and children, and a smattering of men, the old and infirm, the unemployed. Something clutched his chest and passed. So long as the women and kids were in the majority, ridiculous though it was, he felt reassured.

Mazibuko let go of the plan and it skittered into a roll on the bonnet.

Egan unfurled it irritably and pinned one end under a windscreen wiper. Mazibuko had turned away to talk to someone in the crowd, an uncommonly fat woman, loud and gesticulating, waving her arms around. There was a smell in the air, a chokingly familiar sweetness, which Egan recognized as Johnson's Baby Powder. It was coming off the fat woman, from the damp underarms of her floral dress, like the embodiment of her vehemence.

He left the plan to roll itself up again and turned to Mazibuko. 'What's the problem?'

'She's complaining about her house. She says everything is wrong with it. *Everything*.'

Mazibuko's tone was tolerantly amused, but Egan's heart sank. It was always the same. Wherever you went in the townships – although you weren't supposed to call them that any more – in the former townships, in the black areas, when people saw a man with a clipboard or a blueprint, they assumed he was collecting complaints. There was no point in running away. On his last trip to Mpumalanga, the junior planner who was driving him around had convinced him that the best thing was to listen to people. It gave residents the feeling that their problems were being taken seriously and it gave councillors a chance to lend a sympathetic ear. It was a win-win situation, he said. It might even be of advantage to Egan, Gessing and Malan, Sanitary Engineering Consultants. 'Perhaps you'll learn something from the people who actually use your products.'

'We don't make toilet seats. We're responsible for the reticulation system. We're engineers, not bloody plumbers.'

But the planner had been insistent. 'Think of it as public relations.'

'We don't have relations with the public. We have relations with local governments.'

'Then think of it as doing your bit for reconciliation.'

That seemed to be the end point of every exchange. Reconciliation. A conversation stopper.

The fat woman was stamping her foot and raising a cloud of dust.

'What does she want?'

'She wants us to take a look at her house.'

Egan did not even bother to argue. He shoved the plan through the window into the back of the car, took out his briefcase – might as well remove temptation and look official – and followed Mazibuko and the woman into her yard. As he went through the gate, he heard liquid sloshing inside the case. The bottle of Johnnie Walker he'd brought for Louis Bhengu. Brightly gift-wrapped, with a card addressed to the town clerk. He must remember to give it to Mazibuko, he could pass it on to his boss.

The woman opened the door of her house and went inside. Mazibuko stopped on the threshold, leaned in, looked left and right, like someone at a zebra crossing, and followed her.

Egan paused, with a little crowd of women and children around him. There was a crack through the wall of the house so wide he could see through it. It started in the foundations, at the bottom of the doorframe, ran up to the left-hand corner of the lintel, and then zigzagged to the rafters, disappearing beneath the eaves. The overhang was too slight, he noticed in passing, and there were no gutters. They would have trouble with rainwater sooner or later. But how had such a crack appeared in a brand-new structure? There were still fresh spatters of whitewash on the red earth at the foot of the wall, lying brightly in the dust like counters from a board game, among lumps of doughy plaster in kindergarten shapes left over from the building. He would have to explain that walls and floors and doors had nothing to do with him. A child tugged at the clasp of his briefcase, as if Daddy was home from the office with some promised treat, and now he wished that he'd left it in the boot. It made him feel foolish. They would expect him to open it. Perhaps he should give the fat woman the bottle of whisky; that would be a new departure.

He went inside. The lounge was cramped and dark. He saw that the window was half-covered by a dresser, an enormous assembly of beige veneer and silver piping that looked somehow like a vehicle, like a truck parked in that end of the room. Chairs in powder-blue velveteen, an old-fashioned coffee table with ball-and-claw legs, muscularly bulging, a chromium lampstand, a vase in the shape of a swan. The table looked like it was about to spring on him.

The fat woman was pacing out the dimensions of the room, banging into the furnishings and making them wobble. What a performance, Egan thought. And at that instant, as if a flashbulb had gone off in his own mind, the photographer in the doorway opposite pressed his shutter and leapt into focus.

What's *he* doing here? Egan blinked the glare out of his eyes. Noticed now that the sofa on the darkest side of the room was occupied: two men, side by side, both bearded, both wearing black leather jackets. Mazibuko was squatting to talk to them. They must have been waiting here all along.

Mazibuko beckoned him to join them, and the two men stood up. Ramaramela and Marakabane, Chairman and Treasurer respectively of the Residents' Association. Good men, Mazibuko said, aside. Ramaramela, Marakabane. They looked very alike to Egan, possibly brothers. But then surely they would have the same name? It was probably just his usual weakness: he did not have a memory for faces. Or names. He made a mental note that Ramaramela was wearing a charm at his neck in the shape of an animal. While they were shaking hands, with the ritual thumb-clasping that always made him feel like a schoolboy playing at being a spy, the man with the camera crept closer and the flashbulb popped again.

'What's this?'

'Oh, they're doing a piece on the housing question. Delivery.'

'Who exactly?'

'Hang on a second.' Mazibuko turned away to watch the fat woman going backwards and forwards through a doorway, glancing off the doorposts, keeping up a running commentary. A single word kept leaping out of the flow: *fucked*. Uttered so bitterly, with such italic emphasis it was almost comical, and Egan had to suppress a laugh.

'Mrs Ntlaka says the doorways are too narrow.' When Mazibuko spoke near his ear, Egan smelt booze on his breath.

Mrs Ntlaka came back carrying a grass broom. She knocked against the roof with the end of the handle, a little storm of dust sifted down, the camera flashed, she said *fucked* several times, as if she was spitting out pips, she went back through the doorway, banging from pillar to post like a medicine ball.

'She says there is no ceiling.'

'I get the idea.'

'Let's go through.'

Mazibuko took Egan's elbow and guided him into the next room.

There were two beds pushed together. Queen-size, Egan thought. A dressing table packed with shiny things, bottles and animals, a porcelain woman with a parasol, more swans. There was not much room to pace in here but Mrs Ntlaka was managing, making the room shudder, flinging her vibrating arms into the air as if she wanted to get rid of them, intent on demonstrating that she did not fit in her home. Was she trying to knock something over? Would she persist until she had smashed one of the ugly ducklings into pieces of evidence?

Fucked resounded. She clearly had no sense of the power of the expletive. Despite the stagy vehemence, she might just as well have been saying something innocuous, like *on the blink*. The incongruity of it had brought a smile to Mazibuko's lips, a trace of sympathy. The man with the camera was moving around energetically, appreciatively, raising the ancient-looking contraption with its big silver mixing-bowl of a flash, waving it at Mrs Ntlaka, like a creature communicating with its proboscis. How odd it is, Egan thought, that outdated technologies always put one in mind of insects or kitchens.

Taking Mazibuko's cue, Egan fixed a concerned frown to his

face. Unreasonable thoughts ran through his mind. If she's so hard done by, so deprived, why the hell is she so fat? Hasn't it occurred to her that she's too big for the house? Isn't it better than living in a shack anyway? Does she need reminding what a really *fucked* structure looks like? He should give her the talk about counting her blessings, about losing some weight. But the photographer was hovering, buzzing in and out, trying to find his focus, and Egan swallowed his anger. Eating shit again. Now the flash wouldn't go off. Mrs Ntlaka, having just flounced out of the room very effectively, came back, flounced again, and was even better the second time round.

'You must be in this one.'

Mazibuko took Egan by the elbow again, but he shrugged him loose, and they walked one after the other into the passageway. Were the two of them related? Egan wondered, at the sight of the little man's roly-poly backside. Mazibuko and Mrs Ntlaka were fat in the same way, they bulged in identical places. It wouldn't surprise him to learn that they were brother and sister. The door at the end of the passage opened into the toilet. Mrs Ntlaka was settling herself on the toilet seat, about to demonstrate what was wrong with it. But Egan, though he was no plumber, did not need a demonstration. The toilet was too high. Instead of being set straight into the floor, the bowl had been elevated on a cement plinth. The seat would have reached to mid-thigh on a man as tall as himself. What on earth was the contractor thinking? It might have suited a giant, one of those American basketball players, Shaquille O'Neal. The Shaq Attack.

Mrs Ntlaka sat on the toilet with her feet dangling. She had the same disproportionately tiny feet as Mazibuko, in the same clumpy shoes, a pair of boy's school shoes, sturdy brown-leather lace-ups. How had Mazibuko put it? A throne at the end of the passage...She hardly looked regal. A queen on the stool.

Mazibuko's hand pressed in the small of Egan's back, propelling him forward. He squeezed into the narrow space beside Mrs Ntlaka, with his hand resting on top of the cistern. Mazibuko squeezed into the space opposite. The room smelt of talcum powder and roses. The rose smell was coming from a crocheted poodle on the window sill. A toilet-roll holder. The dog's puffy body parts must be stuffed with pot-pourri. Ramaramela and Marakabane squashed into the little room too and sank down on their haunches in front like football players. The team. I must look like the physiotherapist, with my briefcase, Egan thought. The physiotherapist was always white, even when all the players were black. Or do I look like the ambassador from a foreign country come to present his credentials?

He looked past the photographer, hunched over the camera as if he were hooded in black, at the bank of laughing faces in the passage.

The photographer was not satisfied with the pose. He rearranged the two men from the Residents' Association – the squatters, Egan thought wryly – flattening them against the walls on either side, so that the marvellous gap between the soles of Mrs Ntlaka's shoes and the cement floor would be apparent. Then he scurried back into position and pressed the shutter.

When they finally left, Egan discovered that his steering lock was jammed. It was an Eagle Claw, endorsed by the AA, supposedly unpickable. But Mrs Ntlaka called an ageing Young Lion from the house next door and he picked it in a minute with a Swiss Army knife and a length of wire.

Mazibuko dropped him back at his hotel and said he would call for him again in a couple of hours. They were going out for dinner. This time Mr Bhengu would definitely be joining them.

In the room, Egan took the whisky out of his briefcase. It had gone right out of his mind until now. Spitefully, he tore off the garish wrapping paper and opened the bottle. Bugger Mr Bhengu. He fetched a glass from the bathroom, took it out of its plastic wrapper, and poured himself a stiff double. Probably a bad idea on an empty stomach. Bugger that too.

As he crumpled up the paper to throw it away the pattern snagged his eye. For God's sake. A host of little fuckers, a gifts-and-novelties Kama Sutra. Must be some *Cosmo* promotion or other. All along he'd assumed they were Bushman figures, motifs from rock paintings. He'd give Estelle a flea in her ear when he got back to the office. What if he'd given this to Bhengu? Never mind Mrs Ntlaka.

He tilted the bottle again, turning a double into a triple, and called Janine. He could hear the kids in the background, listening to something noisy on the television, too engrossed to come to the phone. He told her about Mrs Ntlaka.

'Moaning,' she sympathized. 'The national sport.'

'It's the old problem of expectations. People want too much. They're unrealistic.'

'Blame the plans.' Spoken with a touch of irony.

It was something he always said. 'Blame the plans, shoot the planners.' And as usual when he heard his own reasonable contentions in someone else's mouth, he became defensive, he switched sides. 'Well, they have a point, most of the time. The paint's not dry and the houses are already falling apart. But sometimes you wish people would just shut up and make the best of things. This Mrs Ntlaka was such a drama queen.'

He told her about the *fucked* monologue and the photograph in the toilet.

'Sounds hilarious. From here.'

'It was infuriating.'

'Sorry.'

'I just wish I knew what it was all about. Why did Mazibuko make an arrangement with these characters from the Residents' Association? Rama-what-have-you and his twin. Sort of secretively. Why didn't he tell me about it in advance? Instead of setting the whole thing up and then pretending it was all a big coincidence. Who stands to gain? I tried to speak to him about it, to let him know in a subtle way that I was on to him, but he clammed up. I keep getting the feeling that he only tells me what I want to hear.'

'Which is?'

'God knows.'

'So where are you going for dinner?'

'He wouldn't let on. He just said it would be something different. An experience.'

'Probably a shebeen.'

'Again.'

'Or maybe a roast-mealie stall on a street corner somewhere?'

'I'm hoping. It'll be a change from having people piss on your shoes in the name of cultural exchange.'

After they'd rung off, he realized that he'd forgotten the most important thing. It was the whole reason he was so irritated. The cracks in the walls and the missing ceilings had nothing to do with him. He was a sanitary engineer. And there was nothing wrong with the sewage system, they could say what they liked. He should call her back and tell her. But, of course, she knew all this already.

Actually, what he needed was a shower. He was reeking, his hair was full of dust, his armpits were itching, but he felt so weary he could hardly move his limbs. He pulled off his shoes and lay on the bed with his fingers laced behind his head.

A few years back, he'd done some work with a black architect on a low-cost development in Cape Town. It was quite unusual in those days, practically unheard-of. Once, as they were looking over the project together, Meintjies had put his finger down on the plan.

'There's only one problem with this township of ours. All the people are white.'

'Can you really tell?'

As if it's my fault, Egan thought. He was on the point of making a defence. People were obsessed with race, he was sick of it. But when he took a closer look at the figures dotted about on the drawings, he saw that Meintjies was right. The race of these stock figures, these little loiterers and passers-by, was apparent less in the obvious features, like their paper-white skin or ruler-straight hair, than in their styles, their attitudes. The man in the checked jacket sitting on a park bench with his legs crossed, reading the newspaper; the woman walking her dog, the hem of her skirt folded around her calves by the breeze, a scarf – this was patently a scarf rather than a *doek* – tied under her chin; the little girl on a bicycle with training wheels. They were not just white, they were European. The benches looked French, the lampposts Italian. Was it possible? Shouldn't everything be American? But no, there was a European signature on the plans. Perhaps that was half the reason people were so disappointed in the reality? Letraset or someone should produce a line of black people, of *poor* black people, a couple of waxy sheets of barefoot street children, barbers with oilcan chairs, coat-hanger hawkers, scrap-metal merchants with supermarket trolleys full of stolen manhole covers. Why not braziers, bricks, rickety wooden benches hammered together out of packing-case pine, instead of this wrought-iron street furniture that made every corner of the world look like Green Park or the Tiergarten? What did Dewar call it? 'Low-cost clip-on infrastructure.' You mean benches? Egan had asked him at the last conference. You mean bus shelters? Let's get real. Let's have more realism at the planning stage. That's what you need if you're going to do your bit for reconstruction and development. Realism.

The Madiba shirt was a mistake. He'd decided to go casual, although the loose-fitting shirt with its African design –

argumentative little people jumping up and down waving their arms in the air, jagged lines sparking from their fists – always made him feel ridiculous. It was a bit like Estelle's wrapping paper, he thought sourly. He should have gone with his instincts and worn a suit. That's the tone Louis Bhengu set: a dark blue business suit and a red tie. Bhengu got out of the minibus, which was idling under the canopy at the hotel entrance, to greet his guest. Mazibuko made the introductions and they shook hands. Then Mazibuko opened the sliding door of the bus, a sleek sixteen-seater with tinted windows, and guided Egan into the interior.

He was surprised to find two men lounging in the back seats, less surprised that they were Ramaramela and Marakabane of the Residents' Association. They leaned forward at the same moment to shake his hand. They had both discarded their leather jackets in favour of suits, old-gold for Ramaramela, petrol-blue for Marakabane. The Madiba shirt felt even sillier. If he hadn't got dressed in such a hurry he might have thought better of it! He quelled his discomfort and tried to fix each man's name in his memory. Ramaramela, Rama, yellow margarine. Yellow Ramaramela. Marakabane was blue. Blue like a marabou. Was a marabou blue? It didn't really matter. Blue Marakabane. Yellow Ramaramela, Blue Marakabane.

Bhengu slid into the passenger seat in front, beside Mazibuko, and they drove away from the hotel. It was a while since Egan had been in a vehicle he wasn't driving. He could sense the two men in the seats behind him, although no one spoke. For a moment, he felt like a child on a family outing.

He'd been asleep when they called for him, and dreaming about Nicholas, his son. The dream came back to him now, as he moistened the tip of his forefinger with spittle and surreptitiously cleaned the sleep out of the corners of his eyes. Nicky was playing on the floor of the nursery, Egan was kneeling beside him, scattered between them was a set of coloured plastic rings that had to be fitted over a peg to form a cone. An educational toy. Nicky wanted the big ring that belonged at the base of the cone but it was out of reach. As he teetered on his padded backside, Egan picked up the ring that lay at his knee and handed it to him. It was just a plastic ring. And yet it was also the 48 per cent of South Africans who lived below the poverty line. Not an image of them, not a symbol, not even an idea. The thing itself, somehow, the poverty. But that was also just a word, and this was just a piece of plastic, a coloured quoit. Nicky took it in his chubby fingers, banged it against the peg and slid it down to the bottom. The toy was perfectly harmless. That was one of the selling points: no sharp edges, nothing a child could hurt himself with or choke on. It developed motor skills, perceptual skills, judgements about scale and colour. Hand, eye. Egan reached for the red ring, the second largest one. People were always commenting how Nicky's hands, tiny as they were, were so much like his father's: the same pronounced curve to the ring finger, the same square nails. In Egan's own adult fingers, the red ring was the 40 per cent of South Africans who had access to running water. His hands were wet with them. He tried to slide the ring over the peg but it would not fit. Nicky pushed the ring away and put the small yellow one over the peg. It dropped to the bottom where it did not belong. The 19 per cent who were HIV positive. Or was it the 35 per cent who had access to telephones? Egan slid it off again. Nicky grabbed at it. The child's hands, tender prophecies of his father's – the only feature of his own body he had once thought attractive, spoilt now by age and use, hardened and coarsened, with hairs curling out of the knuckles, more and more of them as he got older, wrinkled, scarred, veined – the pudgy little fingers were surprisingly powerful. They jerked the ring away.

And then it was the telephone ringing: the receptionist to say that a Mr Mazibuko was waiting for him in the lobby.

Bra Zama's African Eatery was in a peri-urban no-man's-land, where a dying business district petered out in motor town, to judge by the number of used-car dealers in the dimly lit block they had just travelled down. There was a branch of Something Fishy on the other side of the intersection, a retread shop, a couple of nameless businesses with their windows obscured by grilles. As they pulled into the parking lot, Egan had a fleeting impression of carved wooden posts and thatch. A nightwatchman, dressed in a greatcoat and a balaclava despite the summer heat, came to attention and saluted them, ironically perhaps, and then slumped back into a garden chair under a floodlight against the corrugated-iron fence.

Coals were glowing in rusty braziers on either side of the entrance and they passed through this fiery gauntlet into the interior, where a man in a bubu, with his elbows propped on a 44-gallon drum, stood ready to receive them. The wall behind him was papered entirely in packaging, like the inside of a shack, Glenryck Pilchards and Motorola phones, while the walls to left and right were dotted with African masks. It was a clever bit of décor. Even now, with only half the tables occupied, there was an air of expectant busyness about the place.

Bhengu was known to the manager. He led them at once to a table in the middle of the room where another man sat waiting with a bottle of beer in front of him, a very dark man with hooded eyes and a shaved head. Egan wondered whether he had shaved his hair just to show off the scars that covered his skull, like those youngsters who had to wear vests all the time so that people could see their tattooed arms. Mazibuko made the introductions and they all sat down. A kitchen table, covered in oilcloth that stuck to Egan's forearms, chairs of curved chrome and Formica, insistently nineteen-fifties.

Mazibuko was right, Egan thought, it was going to be an *experience*. And he had an odd sense that it would be a significant experience too, that he would remember this evening, that he would look back on it. He could already see himself looking back on it, from a tremendous distance, and understanding, at last, what it was all about. He wished he was there now, at that reassuring remove, on a height, filled with the wisdom of hindsight.

A statuesque woman, elongated by a knotted head cloth and platform shoes, brought the menus. She said her name was Miriam and that she would be their waitress for the evening. She began to recite the 'specials': lamb breyani, nyama ya figo, beef stewed the Nigerian way. The waitresses must have to learn the specials by heart, he thought, like actors. A necessary part of the training. He made a mental note of the LM prawns, drew a line through it. Lourenço Marques smacked of colonialism. He should have something more adventurous, something equatorial. Pounded yam, perhaps. He would ask what was in the chicken egusi, which went with it. While Miriam was speaking, he examined her costume. She was clearly *in costume*, dressed up as something, although he wasn't sure what. Some national costume or other. Nigerian, say. Or was she supposed to be a shebeen queen?

She took the drinks order and left them to consider their options.

The menu was bound in metal: beer tins beaten flat and stapled together into a patchwork. You were not meant to leaf through it until something caught your fancy; you were meant to read it like a children's book, for your amusement and education. It was part of the experience. What struck him forcefully, because it had been picked out in red letters on every page, was the phrase: 'New South Africa'. How dated it seemed. When had it been coined? Five years ago? Already it was worn out and passing quietly from use.

He turned with a clank to the top of page one. He was embarking upon a sensory safari, the menu said, unimaginable tastes and smells were in store for him. He would have the opportunity of savouring a range of authentic delicacies, from the warm heart of the countryside to the cool tang of the city streets, from Zulu kebabs to Xhosa dumplings, from Ugandan risi bisi to Malawian paella, from Ma Zama's fatcakes to Bra Zama's chakalaka chicken. What the hell was that?

'The beef is good.' It was the first time Bhengu had addressed him directly.

'Actually, I was thinking of trying the umfino.' One of the few dishes on the menu he had recognized.

'No, no, no.' The name of the fifth man had already slipped from Egan's mind. He stretched out his hand with the palm turned down and tilted it from side to side. 'It is a city version.'

'They don't make it the traditional way?'

'No, it is very good. It is better than my wife's.'

They all laughed.

'Perhaps I'll try it then.'

'No, no, no. You will not like it.'

'You will be complaining, "What is this?"'

More laughter.

'Also.' Marakabane tapped on the metal cover of the menu with his forefinger. 'You must not have the ulusu lwegusha.'

'What's that?' He looked for it in the pages.

'It is the stomach of a sheep.'

'Tripe.'

'It will make you sick.'

'I've eaten tripe before. My mother used to cook it quite often when I was a kid. Because it was cheap. I always thought it was delicious.'

'Ulusu, ulusu.' Marakabane seemed to be mulling over an entirely different foodstuff, something loosely coiled and heavy with blood.

'You must have the beef,' Bhengu said.

'With the Afritude Sauce,' Mazibuko added.

Egan looked for the Afritude Sauce on the menu. Again he wished he was in that faraway place, the future, looking back.

'The Afritude Sauce is the speciality of the house,' Bhengu was reading off the menu. 'It is the flavour of the New South Africa, an exhilarating blend of earthy goodness and spicy sophistication.' He waved to the waitress.

'It is the real thing,' said Marakabane.

'In that case, I suppose I'll try it.'

Bhengu smiled at him indulgently.

Miriam came with the drinks. There were two bottles of white wine in a plastic bucket, four quarts of Castle lager, two quarts of milk stout, and a clattering fistful of enamel mugs.

They ordered in Sotho. Bhengu ordered for Egan. The only two words in the entire exchange he understood were: Afritude Sauce.

Mazibuko uncapped the wine and filled their mugs. 'Mr Bhengu would like to propose a toast.'

Bhengu looked at Egan and said, 'To the Hani View Sewage System.' He pronounced it 'sea-wage'.

They raised their mugs and drank.

They began to speak about Hani View, the progress on the new houses, the problems with the substation, now mercifully resolved, the grading of the roads, the squatters from Hani

View Extension 1 making a nuisance of themselves. The episode with Mrs Ntlaka and the photographer came back to Egan and he thought of bringing it up. But why bother when the mood was so light and cheerful? It was all water under the bridge, so to speak, and he was relieved to be back on common ground.

As they sat there in the middle of the room, the focus of attention, he, Egan, and the five black men, an equal among equals, he became conscious of their special status. They represented something important. They were the only racially mixed party in the place. Glancing around at the other tables, at the pale Danes and Poms, taking a quick census, he felt weirdly proud of himself. He was part of the new order, that part of it that did not need to be labelled 'new'. It even tickled him that he might be part of an 'arrangement' of some kind, something vaguely disreputable. He had to wonder about the cosy relationship between the councillors and the men from the Residents' Association. Who was the fifth man? Was it seemly that they should all be meeting like this? Who would be picking up the tab? But his questions lost their force in the face of a new certainty: this was the way the world worked and there was nothing to be ashamed of. It was all about connections, it was about who you knew, I'll scratch your back, that kind of thing. How did anything ever get done but by such accommodations?

The conversation flowed along smoothly for an hour. They had all night, it went without saying, no reason why the kitchen should rush. They spoke in English, with pinches of Sotho, Zulu and Afrikaans. They deferred to Egan on technical questions. Were they getting their money's worth from Rubicon? Was it true that the zoning laws prevented them from building on Saturday afternoons, but said nothing about surveying? Why could they not lay the pipes for the new houses down by the vlei underneath the existing road? Egan began to feel like one of the boys. He found himself referring to them as 'gents'. He ordered another bottle of wine. The empties in the ice-water had sloughed their labels, so he didn't know what they were drinking, but Ramaramela said he should ask for the poeswyn, it would do, and they all laughed.

When the wine came, Egan filled up their mugs. 'Have another dop, gents.'

They had finished the new bottle before Miriam brought the food. Bhengu said it was time to move on to beer anyway. You couldn't drink wine all evening.

The fifth man had ordered the tripe. It looked nothing like the dish Egan remembered from his childhood and he was glad he had been dissuaded from trying it. There were pieces of spongy tissue in it like something out of the pathology lab. The other four were eating the same big platters of roasted meat. No sign of a skewer, so it couldn't be the Zulu kebabs. Looked like chops, your basic braaivleis. Was it even on the menu? You probably had to know someone in the kitchen. Perfect, he thought, the one thing everyone wants isn't even mentioned in the small print.

The Afritude Sauce came in a calabash propped in a wire stand. It was an unappetizing yellow and had bits of peanut and leafy green stuff floating in it. It looked lumpy, half-digested, stewed in its own juices. But when he tasted a bit on the end of his knife it turned out to be delicious. He spooned it over his steak.

They ate.

Slowly, peristaltically, Egan felt himself moving to the edge of the conversation. They were talking mainly in Sotho now, switching back into English occasionally to include him. The man with the scarred head mentioned the new houses (Egan guessed they were the ones he'd seen that morning).

Ramaramela and Marakabane assured him that they were looking after their 'constituency'. They said several times that they would 'bring their people along', as if they were talking about their families. Egan made a point about the floodline. Bhengu agreed with him. Then they slipped back into Sotho. What were they talking about? Leaning back in his chair to claim the first half metre of that distance he craved so much, studying their expressions, their gestures, their tones, the way their heads inclined towards one another as they spoke, he began to suspect that *nothing* important was being discussed with him. That the real purpose of the exchange, in which he appeared to be an equal partner, was in the sidelong chatter, the small talk he didn't understand. It was possible, wasn't it? That everything that mattered lay between the lines? There was something conspiratorial in the air; he would almost have said in the décor. But how to be sure? This unease he was feeling might just as well be insecurity, anxiety, even a guilty conscience. Why should he feel excluded? Wasn't that a sign of weakness in itself?

A fantasy: if he could listen in patiently on everything they didn't want him to know, he would be able to turn the tables. He remembered those stories about South Africans abroad speaking Afrikaans at a dinner party, secure in the knowledge that no one would understand them, being nasty about the company, passing comments about the food – only to find that their host had grown up in Potch and spoke Afrikaans perfectly. He imagined himself at the end of this evening, as they were parting in the soothingly lit lobby of the hotel, putting out a hand to Louis Bhengu and saying in perfect Sotho, 'Well, gentlemen, thank you for a very entertaining evening.' But he couldn't even guess at the shape of the words in his mouth.

Miriam appeared. Everything all right?

'Fine, fine.'

The steak was tough, he thought, but the sauce did wonders for it. He added another couple of spoonfuls.

Then he took a closer look at the décor. There was a bicycle with square wheels suspended over the bar counter, which was faced with corrugated iron. He had seen something similar in a pub once, one of those Irish chains, a McGinty's or what have you. Perhaps they'd got the idea there. Barbed wire in the rafters. These wooden masks everywhere, with their poppy eyes and round surprised mouths that were just made to hold a blowpipe, their bulging foreheads and scarred cheeks. They gave him a peculiar sense of being watched, as if a crowd of hungry tribesmen were staring at him while he tried to eat, gawking as if they had never seen a white man before.

The masks were nearly identical, yet each one had something individual about it, in addition to its ritual mutilations, as if they were all finally related, cousins, second cousins, the members of one intricate, impossibly extended family.

Perhaps it was not that different with Ramaramela and Marakabane. Ramaramela yellow, Marakabane blue. Why did he find it so difficult to tell them apart? They both looked like gangsters to him, like those identikit portraits of heist suspects or hijackers. The same interchangeable features. No matter how hard the artist worked at giving each an identity, choosing carefully from among the hundreds of eyes and noses and mouths, they ended up resembling one another. They were faces that had never been lived in. They were always completely symmetrical and relentlessly typical. In their own way, they were flawless.

The Michael Jackson joke someone had circulated by email came back to him. How does Michael Jackson pick his nose? With a catalogue. He thought of telling it, decided against. What status would Michael Jackson have in this company? Would he be a figure of fun? A role model? He couldn't say.

In any event, he could not interrupt their conversation to tell a joke. They were talking heatedly. He had the feeling that for the first time this evening he had ceased to matter to them. It made no difference that he was there. The thought had hardly crossed his mind when Bhengu leaned over without missing a beat and stuck his spoon in the Afritude Sauce. At first, Egan thought he was helping himself. Instead, he gave the contents of the little calabash a stir, tipped several spoonfuls over Egan's steak, licked the spoon, raised his eyebrows appreciatively, and went on talking.

Egan drained his mug and considered the gesture. What did it mean? Was it a sign of sharing, of hospitality? Like the good host topping up his guest's glass. Or was he being ridiculed? Why did he even think this was a possibility? He could no longer tell the difference between kindness and cruelty. Every day he found himself wondering whether people were being nice to him or taking the mickey.

Suddenly he felt exhausted and drunk. Poeswyn and milk stout, not to mention a third of whisky in the afternoon. He should never have opened that bottle, he should have given it to Bhengu. He focused on the men across the table. Which one was Ramaramela? They had taken off their jackets and slung them over the backs of their chairs. Perhaps they'd changed places? They had all made several trips to the toilet.

Ramaramela might have sat down in Marakabane's chair. Ramaramela yellow, Marakabane blue. Or vice versa. He'd lost the rhythm of it. Which one was the caribou? Their names had detached themselves from their faces, from their clothes, from their colours, and he simply could not put them together again. Their voices kept slipping sideways too, like subtitles in a film. Marakabane – was it? – went on talking, his lips were moving, his eyebrows waggling, yet his words seemed to hover in front of Ramaramela's mouth.

His eyes wandered from the faces of his companions to the masks on the walls. There seemed to be more and more of them. Multipliers. He felt surrounded. It was uncannily like a white South African nightmare, he thought. An *old* one. As if they were in a glass house, feasting, while the hordes outside pressed their hungry faces to the walls.

Margarine. He would just have to take a look at Ramaramela's trousers. He stood up. As if that had been a signal, the lights dimmed, music blared and a troupe of gumboot dancers burst through the armour-plated doors of the kitchen. The one in front was the manager, the man in the bubu, who had shown them to their table.

There were masks in the men's room too, suspended from the tiles above each urinal. While Egan pissed, he was compelled to gaze into a wooden face, which reflected exactly his own expression of glazed relief. Alongside each mask was a sign advertising condoms or hands-free telephones. There were more masks between the mirrors above the washbasins, all terribly scarred and battered, staring at him with disbelief. He looked ridiculous in this shirt. He looked like Denis fucking Beckett. He'd been tucking his shirt into his pants since he was a kid: now suddenly it was a sign that he was 'uptight'. You were supposed to let it all hang out, starting with your shirt tails. Bugger that. Bugger *them*. He loosened his belt and tucked his shirt into the sides of his underpants, the way he'd always done it. That's better.

When he got back to the table, the gumboot dancing was over and they were ordering dessert. Without even waiting for encouragement, he said he would have the rainbow cake, with ice cream.

When Miriam brought the bill, the fifth man insisted on paying and dropped a credit card on the saucer. Egan protested half-heartedly, accepted the offer, insisted on putting in for the tip.

While he picked through the change in his wallet, he was reminded of the joke about Van der Merwe visiting the Empire State Building. Looking down from the viewing platform at the top, he sees a quarter lying on the sidewalk. So he runs all the way down to the street to pick it up – and finds that it's a manhole cover. He was full of jokes this evening. For a moment, he actually considered telling this one. Then he imagined Janine rolling her eyes: there was a certain kind of humour, she always said, and it wasn't necessarily lavatorial, that was appreciated only by sanitary engineers.

Egan slid the metal clamp of the shower attachment up on the bar for the tenth time and fastened the screw. The thing wouldn't stay put. He shut his eyes and thrust his face into the jet, letting the water sluice off him, washing away the dust and sweat of the day, rinsing off the insults, real and imagined, the glare of cheap publicity, the sea-wage, Mrs Ntlaka's talcum powder, Bra Zama's Afritude Sauce. He detached the shower from the clamp and played the jet idly over his balls. It was a pleasant feeling, the warm water prickling on his skin, but then the flow suddenly ran cold again. He reached through the curtain for his watch on the cistern. Twenty minutes before *Raging Bull* started. He turned off the taps and got out of the shower.

He went through to the room with a towel around his waist and switched on the TV. A filler of some kind, an infomercial, a muscular woman walking in an exercise machine. Close-ups of her ridged abdomen, her sinewy arms. Hardness. A quality that had not always been associated with women. Once they had cultivated softness; now they were for such hard-edged definitions. American women were leading the way. They even seemed to take pride in the precise lines at the sides of their mouths. He turned the sound down. He unwrapped the chocolate that he'd found on his pillow when he came in from dinner and ate it. He poured himself another whisky from Bhengu's bottle, scaled it up to a double, a triple. Then he lay back on the bed to wait for the movie.

The usual stack of cards and pamphlets was on the bedside table, and he flipped through them. The TV guide. The services – laundry, shoeshine, car rental. Wake-up calls. The room-service menu. At the bottom of the stack, mixed up with the writing paper, was a complaints questionnaire. Please take the time to complete this questionnaire before your departure, it said. It will help us to improve our service. Your needs are important to us. Strangely enough, someone had already taken up the challenge. Mr J. P. van der Haas of Rotterdam.

He had covered the whole form in tiny print. Presumably the chambermaid should have taken it away for 'processing', but it had slipped in among the other papers and been overlooked.

Egan propped himself more comfortably against the pillows and considered the form. It was dated at the top: the night before. There was always something unsettling about hotel rooms, when you thought about it. A long line of strangers slouching about on the same furniture as if it belonged to them. Usually you did not know their names, every identifiable trace of them had been erased – the sweat, the cigarette smoke, the scuffing and scraping were unavoidable but generalized – and so it did not bother you much. This was too close for comfort. He could imagine Van der Haas lying here just twenty-four hours ago, exactly where he was lying now, with his spiky Dutch hair resting against the same spot on the plush headboard, his forehead postmarked with resentment, his stockinged ankles crossed, the big toe of one foot scratching the instep of the other, and the ballpoint clutched in his fist.

Apparently Van der Haas had not found much to his liking. Under *General Condition of Room* he had written: 'Bedclothes and carpet worn. Not up to standard of 2 star hotel.' Then there was an asterisk that guided Egan to a note at the bottom of the page, where Van der Haas's signature was coiled like a pubic hair in a bar of soap: 'Decor itself is old-fashioned. Depressing. It is time to redecorate. One feels one to be back in 1978 in this room.'

He got up and switched on the central light. Took in the veneers, the floral lampshades, the reproduction of a bushveld scene over the TV set. *Nightfall at the Waterhole*. The slightly awkward positioning of the chair between the bathroom door and the bed now made sense: it had been put there deliberately to cover a threadbare patch. Suddenly he wished he had slippers. He should put on his socks, at least, to avoid the sticky prickle of the fibres on his bare soles. Extraordinary, he thought, the place is only a couple of years old. The finishes must have been very shoddy to start with or the volume of guests astounding. At the thought of all the strangers who had passed through this cramped space, breathing, dripping, shedding skin, spilling fluids, his stomach tightened. Involuntarily, he put his hand over his mouth.

He had folded the bedspread to the foot of the bed. Perhaps the chambermaid had turned it back in the first place to hide some flaw? Perhaps every homely touch was calculated to conceal something? He opened out the bedspread. Seemed fine. The sheet was a bit grey. He turned over one of the pillows and there, indeed, was a hole in the slip the size of an egg. He swapped it with the pillow on the second bed, which was in better shape.

He turned to the next item on Van der Haas's list. 'Bedside lamp broken.' Must be the one attached to the second bed. He pressed the switch. Nothing. An intolerable pressure began to rise in him, as if every petty irritation he had endured in his life was repeating on him, trying to force its way to the surface. Out of the corner of his eye he saw Robert De Niro, a bloated black-and-white Robert De Niro, speaking to the camera. But Van der Haas was not finished with him. Under *Bathroom facilities* he had no fewer than five numbered complaints. 'One. Shower curtains. Replace with glass.' Egan remembered the way the limp plastic sheet had clung to his back, sucked in by the steam. 'Two. Shower attachment broken. Three. Dots on taps wrong way round. Green = cold, Red = hot.' No wonder he'd scalded himself. 'Four. Plug doesn't fit.' He went through to the bathroom. The pants he had put in to soak lay damply in the bottom of the empty basin. Why on earth had he put them in water anyway? He should have taken them home to clean. Must have been drunk. He should stick them in the trouser press. In the Hosenbügler. If the bloody thing was working.

Vinegar surged in his throat, peanuts, garlic, that stinkbug herb thing. Jesus. He flung himself down on the bed with the questionnaire in his hand. He couldn't bear to go on. Fucking Van der Haas. He thumbed the volume button on the remote but nothing happened. Probably also on the Dutchman's list. A skinnier Robert De Niro was having the crap beaten out of him now, sweat sprayed off his battered head, cursive exclamations of blood and saliva trailed from his broken mouth. Egan drew his knees up protectively and cupped his hands between his legs. Even without the sound, he could hear fists thudding on flesh and bone.

CURIOUSER

In the studio attached to his house, where he usually engaged in the serious business of making art, 'S. Majara', indulging a whim, began to construct a lantern out of wooden masks. The four he had chosen for this purpose lay in sequence on the floor beneath the windows. Many others were scattered around the tall white room, leaning against walls and lying on trestle tables, pinning down the clutter like oversized paperweights. Besides masks, there were wooden animals arranged in groups on the windowsills and the seats of chairs, carvings of buck and zebra and elephant of the kind displayed for sale to tourists by hawkers all over the city. Curios. The meat of *Curiouser*.

'S. Majara' was having a closing. It was the new thing, more fun than an opening, they said. His show at the Pollak had just come down, he had spent the whole day taking the works apart and packing them up, and the last thing he felt like was a party. But it had to be done.

He put two masks together with their temples touching and aligned the holes he had drilled in their ears. Then he pushed the end of a length of wire through a pierced lobe, bent it sharply and pushed it back through the ear of its neighbour, and twisted the ends together with a pair of pliers. He had an enormous supply of these things. He had begun to think he would never see the end of them.

The third of the lucky foursome had peculiar ears, little lugs tucked into the angles of its jaw – a real lantern jaw, he thought – and the holes he had drilled were useless. He made a new mark with a pencil and carried the mask to the workbench. As he pressed the bit against its forehead, he studied its expression. You could imagine that it was gritting its teeth – but that was just the effect of the drill. If you took the bit out of the picture, the grimace turned to a grin.

The face of Africa, he thought, the one made familiar by ethnographic museums and galleries of modern art, B-grade movies and souvenir shops. Everywhere you went in Johannesburg, wooden faces looked up at you from the pavements at the hawkers' stalls, a running catalogue of expressions that ranged between hollowed-out hunger and plump self-satisfaction, each flipping over into its opposite as soon as the weather changed.

Curiouser had been a great success, a new beginning for him, everyone said so. The *Genocide* series had led them to expect another video installation. Instead he had given them sculpture, witty pieces quite unlike his stock-in-trade. Even people who were habitually sarcastic about his work thought he had achieved something remarkable, liberating the curio from its stifling form, cutting down to the core of its meaning, that sort of thing.

The lantern was finished: a head with four faces. He carried it out of the studio, across a courtyard cluttered with lumber, bolts of wire mesh, paint tins and other oddments, and into the house.

'Let's take a look.' Ruth was painting her nails at the dining-room table. 'The candles are in the dresser, under the dishcloths.'

He fetched one, set it up inside the lantern and lit it. Then he shut the blinds to get the effect. Perfect.

'Think I'll make a few more to spook the guests.'

'Go for it, Sim. Make ten.'

Simeon was an artist. Everything else followed. He had made his name – 'S. Majara' – with three shows on the theme of genocide.

The first of these, the Holocaust work, had been a little obvious perhaps, overladen with ashes and soot; but the second, the Ahmici series, made everyone sit up and take notice. Its element was bone, ground and splintered and scored, and no one who saw it was unmoved. It made you painfully aware that you were corporeal and mortal. Of course, people were intrigued that a black artist should be dealing with Bosnia, although one critic suggested that he mind his own business. Hadn't he heard of Idi Amin?

In fact, his attention had turned already to a more recent African atrocity. The next show, *Genocide III* – the 'Nyanza Shrouds' as it came to be known – was about Rwanda. Its element was dust. The gallery was saturated with it, quite unintentionally. There was a pale shimmer in the air, on the tiles, sifting imperceptibly from the fabric of his winding sheets. People became aware of it sometimes in the soft lisp of their soles on the gallery floor, or, hours later, when they were back in the full-colour world, in a white smudge on the sleeve of a jacket, as if a soul expiring there had left behind this soap-bubble residue.

He had gone to Nyanza with the idea for *Genocide III* half-formed in his mind, to see the site of the massacre, now preserved as an open-air museum. There were ten or twelve people on the trip, a handful of journalists, a researcher from the European Cultural Foundation, a woman representing a Danish church organization that took in orphans ('Hutus *and* Tutsis'), a couple of tourists. On the drive from Kigali, he sat next to Henk from Groningen. This cross-cultural adventurer, as he called himself, had a special interest in genocide. He had done the major concentration camps in his own backyard (Auschwitz, he said, was still the must-see), the Tuol Sleng Genocide Museum in Phnom Penh, and a five-day drive along the Trail of Tears. This was his first African visit, but South Africa was next on the list.

When Henk finally asked him what he did, Simeon could not bring himself to say he was an artist. The idea made him queasy. It suggested an intolerable common purpose with his fellow traveller, whose bony knee was rubbing against his own. He said he was a journalist and patted his camera bag.

The economies of repetition. Any task got faster and easier as you went along. One of the pleasures of working with your hands lay in finding rhythms and refining sequences, discovering how a given process could best be done. By the time he was busy with the eighth lantern, he'd halved the time it took. Eight? Perhaps he'd got a little carried away. But then the raw material was so plentiful.

The masks had come into his hands by chance a year before. It was startling how one lucky find had changed his artistic course – although the gap between corpses and curios was narrower than people thought. An acquaintance, a woman who framed his prints from time to time, had been commissioned to design the décor at Bra Zama's African Eatery. Deciding that he knew more about authentic African style than she did – he was black, after all, never mind the private-school accent – she had asked for his help. The implications intrigued him, the possibility of erasing another line between his art and his livelihood. And the restaurant itself was perfect, a touristy place on the edge of Germiston where people could pretend they were in a shebeen. It appealed precisely because it was so corny. He had explored this ambiguous charm in his sketches for the interior, seizing on the obvious trappings of the tourist experience and trusting that in the end he would be able to turn them inside out, double them back on themselves, so that they meant something else. That was one of his things. 'Recharging the drained object with meaning,' as Jackie Wetzler once put it in *Business Day*.

He hit on the answer soon enough: Bra Zama's African Eatery would have masks. The budget stretched to no more than a handful at shop prices, but he wanted dozens. So he had driven out to the curio-sellers on Ontdekkers Road and William Nicol Drive, diffuse marketplaces straggling along the verges of suburban roads. His plan was to beat one of them down by 'buying in bulk', but they were surprisingly resistant. They wouldn't even name their suppliers.

He was already toying with the idea of making what he needed from scratch when he met Roger, a Malawian who kept a stall on the pavement outside Flea Market World in Bruma. Yes, he had masks, he said, he had six crates of them.

'Six crates!'

'One thousand rand a box, take it or leave it.'

Excess was always interesting. In a flash, 'S. Majara' was calculating whether the grant money he had left over from the *Genocide III* show was enough to buy the whole lot for himself. He could use them in his own work, the real work, after the Eatery potboiler.

Only when he began to unpack the Malawian's masks in his studio did he realize how many there were. His eye had told him fifty or sixty in the whole consignment, but there were that many in a single crate. Every time he threw out a handful of shredded newsprint, expecting to see the blond pine bottom of the box, he found another layer gazing up as astonished as stowaways. There was something charmed about it, like the bottomless granary in a fable. He had used a few dozen of them at Bra Zama's without making a dent in the supply, and still he had a roomful left at home and an unopened crate in the garage. Ruth was sick of it. She'd be glad to see another handful go.

He picked up a lantern in each hand and went into the house again.

She was sawing through a lettuce now at the kitchen counter.

'I'm just going to put these out.'

'Sandy's arrived. She brought that with her.' Pointing with the knife to a portfolio leaning against the wall.

'What is it?'

'The prints that Tanya hasn't got rid of and a couple of posters.'

'Keepsakes.'

'Also the visitors' book. She says you should take a look. Some hilarious stuff.'

'Is Tanya coming?'

'Says so. Here, take the candles with you.' She looped the handles of a plastic bag over his crooked forefinger.

The pool was vividly blue in the twilight (Ruth had already switched on the underwater lights). A liquid lozenge of California in the crust of Gauteng. There was something about it that thrilled him, something glamorous and electric that produced a current of longing with no definite object. The luminous blue water shifted heavily against the sides of the pool, moving for no apparent reason, unless it was the rotation of the earth itself. Although you didn't see the contents of glasses and cups rocking. And why not? He turned the question over in his mind as he went along the terracotta surround of the pool. He should send it to that Q & A column in the *Mail*. Was it all gravity? The moon? You moved a cup through the air and it sloshed over, with many a slip 'twixt cup and lip, blah blah. But the cup was hurtling through space along with the planet and not so much as a ripple. Those palms should be bent double. His hair should be flying, his cheeks filled to bursting. Dizzy Gillespie. Or a freefaller, a skydiver. *Skydiver I*. A man, me, a man walking down a city street with his hair on end, stiff as quills, his cheeks puffed out, his clothes rattling, while everyone else is strolling along as unruffled as you please. A poppy little piece, very MTV, very *Drumroll*. Earthdiver. Arms outstretched, legs rigid. Another little Guronsan C man like the hero of *Bullet-in*, my photographic series. *Drydiver*!

Their guide in Nyanza was a gaunt, middle-aged man with John Lennon glasses, who had survived the massacre by lying for a day among familiar corpses, pretending to be dead. Death had rubbed off on him, it was there on his skin. He showed them the church, the mass grave and the shed where the bones of victims were piled. Then they were free to wander over the red earth, which seemed to express too obviously the idea that it was drenched in blood, through the shells of buildings, across unmown lawns. Bone. Simeon had used bone before. He needed something else. This red clay was garish.

After a while, he found himself alone outside a building with gaping doors. When he went inside, he saw that it had been a clinic. There were hospital beds, tin cabinets, rails for curtains. The place was eerily quiet and complete, as if the massacre had just taken place. It was easy to imagine patients lying in the beds, and doctors and nurses shouldering through the doors, while the fans revolved overhead.

He went outside again into the glare and then retraced his passage into the clinic, looking through the viewfinder this time. He moved slowly, trying to capture the taking-in of detail, discovering the beds cranked up into fractured angles, the ragged mosquito nets, the dusty medicine measures on bedside cabinets. There was a door in one corner of the ward. Hesitantly, an eye afraid of what it might see next, he pushed through into another room. The dispensary. He swung open the door of a cupboard with his foot, still filming, and locked in surprise on shelves dotted with tubes and jars. The cupboard was full. What had preserved it so completely? The certainty that this place was tainted and these remedies had lost their power.

The plaster bandages were on the bottom shelf. So this was what he had come for. He lingered on them, transfixed.

Finally he put the camera down. He emptied the contents of his bag – sweater, lunch pack from the hotel, mineral water, paperback for the bus ride – into the bottom of the cupboard, packed up as many of the rolled bandages as he could (twenty, it turned out) and covered them with his kikoi.

He was busy with the Polaroid when he heard the driver blowing his hooter, signalling that it was time to go. As he made his way to the bus, he noticed that despite being wrapped in plastic the bandages had left traces of white plaster on his fingertips. Dust. That was it. He stopped and wiped his hands on the grass. He felt no guilt about the theft. He did not even think of it in those terms.

On the journey back to the hotel, he found a seat by himself, avoiding Henk from Groningen, and thought about the work. The road jolted into his head the old wisecrack about applying a Band-aid to a cancer. Yet he clutched the bag as if it held the answer to everything.

He made twenty shrouds, weaving into each of them a single roll of plaster bandage. The catalogue explained that there was one winding sheet for every two hundred people who had been killed in Nyanza; it said nothing about the bandages or their provenance. The film footage was also silent on this subject. The moment when he discovered the bandages in the cupboard – the crux of the whole experience, a genuine revelation, captured without artifice – he excised from the video.

Each shroud bore the impression of a human body, a crying mouth, a twisted arm, a hand raised to ward off a blow. The long white sheets were hung in a dimly lit room like photographs of ghosts.

—

'Hey, Simeon,' Sandy called to him from across the pool. She had arranged the garden furniture around the braai and was running a cloth over the table-top. 'I brought your prints back.'

'Ta.'

'Tanya's coming.'

'I heard. What's the plan for tomorrow?'

'We've got to be there by ten.'

'Damn!'

'James is coming half past eleven, twelve with the bakkie to take the stuff to the office. But we'd better be there early, we've still got to dismantle the vitrines. And a couple of pieces will have to be packed properly.'

'Did you get the bubble wrap?'

'Ja.'

'Ta.'

'James is going to drop the "Skinny Rhinoceros" at Norman Fischhoff's this evening. You know he bought the "Rhinoceros"?'

'We should bank the cheque first.'

'Do you think so?'

'Joking, Sands.'

'What are those?'

'Lanterns.' As he padded across the lawn, he raised the two lanterns shoulder-high to show her. They felt like heads, all of a sudden, swinging from his fists. 'I hear we're making a braai. You should get the fire going.'

'That'll be the day. That's boys' work.'

'What do I know about building fires?'

'It's too early anyway.'

'Whatever you say.'

'Bheki will do it. Or Leon. He's one of those men who can't resist taking over at a braai. One whiff of a charcoal briquette and he'll come running.'

He prowled along a path made of railway sleepers to the street door. Ever since Artslink had called 'S. Majara' a 'Young Lion of the Art Scene' – sarcastically, it's true – Simeon had discovered a feline streak in himself that was hard to suppress. The goatee only made it worse. So did the rubber-soled trainers, which looked more like a superior form of foot than a shoe, as if his body had magically projected its striated musculature onto the surface of his skin. Lately he'd taken to inserting something catlike into his gait, a version of padding, a leonine grace.

Every last image on the Nyanza Shrouds had been modelled on Simeon's own body. It irritated some people. They saw it as vanity that he used himself as the measure of all suffering. Whereas he saw it as the opposite. It was a mark of humility, he said, to take yourself as the template, to immerse yourself in the image of the other like an armature in a sculpture.

He had a knack for publicity, no argument there, but that was a different matter. It was nothing but good business sense, even if it offended people who preferred their artists quiet and self-effacing. Whenever he was accused of superficiality, he took comfort in a private conviction that the work was always received more superficially than it had been created. There was always more to it than met the eye. No one even suspected that the sepulchral dust which was such an integral part of the show – the white patina that clung to everything 'like mortality itself', according to Jackie Wetzler – came from Nyanza. No one would ever know.

Some details of *Genocide III* no longer pleased him, but he was satisfied with the big picture.

Entering the largest room at the Pollak, the visitor was stopped short by footage of Rwanda projected on an enormous screen. The slaughter in Nyanza had not been filmed, of course, but television news crews had come to the area a week later, when corpses still lay sprawled in the streets or heaped against walls, where they had been shoved by bulldozers. There was film of the international peacekeepers pulling out of the country, and battle scenes from other parts of the region featuring jeeps and armoured vehicles. The screen stretched from floor to ceiling, apparently as solid as a wall, blocking off two thirds of the room and dwarfing the viewer.

Simeon had spent days at the gallery watching how people responded. Many turned for relief to the monitor on the left-hand wall, which showed the video footage of Nyanza he had shot himself, slow and silent, a small, manageable world, made touching by its scale. Then they crossed to the right-hand wall, where his Polaroids were quilted together. This undulating square the size of a blanket kept suggesting a landscape or a portrait, a relief map or a figure study, before falling apart into random blocks of jungle texture, clay, bark, the surface of the continent seen from a satellite.

Most people were ready to face the projection again, and stepped back against the third wall to try and see the image whole. At this point some of them actually left, retreating through the door they had entered by without having seen the bulk of the exhibition. But those who had read the reviews or glanced at the floor plan on the price list now approached the screen, looking for the gap that would let them through into the space behind, where the shrouds were displayed. The slit was spanned tight and offset deliberately from the centre to make it harder to find. He loved watching this moment – the drama of the compère stranded on the wrong side of the stage curtains, beating at the fabric, sending panicky darts and ripples over the moving surface, until an arm plunged through the gap, and then the whole body slipped gratefully into the image, swallowed up in it.

The opening of the show had been the usual ironic spectacle. One was always aware of the uncomfortable contrasts, the hacked limbs and bleached skulls, the guests with their glasses of wine, the price tags, the little green and red stickers. By the end of the evening several people had spilled their wine stepping through the gap in the screen and left their palm-prints on the fabric.

The highlight was undoubtedly the performance of the Minister of Culture. She had come to give the opening address – there was some political mileage to be made, South Africa was involved in the peace talks in Rwanda, it was all Tanya's idea – and she arrived in a wheelchair. Officially, she had sprained her ankle playing tennis, but everyone knew she'd been hitting the bottle. There she was, slumped in the chair and looking smaller than usual, rolled out to the microphone against a backdrop of military convoys as if she herself were a war veteran. Her foot in its plaster cast stuck out stiffly like the cannon of a tank. Leon, the painter, Simeon's old university buddy, had leaned over, breathing vinegar and cigarette smoke, and said, 'Shot herself in the foot again…' The *Star*'s critic would remark in his review that the Minister symbolized perfectly the state of art and culture under her administration.

Of course, only 'S. Majara' saw the connection between the plastered foot of the Minister and the powdery shrouds in the room next door, which some people insisted were 'too easy' and she herself was indisposed to view. You could hide a multitude of private jokes in a term like 'mixed media'.

Grace was a concept he considered more and more important for negotiating the world. He had picked it up on Oprah during his years at the Art Institute in Chicago, and he clung to it for that reason. What was that segment of her show called again? 'Remember Your Spirit.' Like a sign saying 'Mind the Step'. Perhaps it was to be expected: the more vulgar everyday life became, and the more overwhelmed people were by craven impulses and base desires, greed and envy, gluttony and lust, the more they reached for the old ideals like generosity and grace. He thought of people in hotel rooms, who knew they should go out for air or open a window, at least, but could not rouse themselves to do it, who turned their faces instead towards wheezing air conditioners and tut-tutting fans.

He put the lanterns down on either side of the door in the garden wall, stood a candle in each one, scraped a match into his palm and carried the flame down to the wicks like a drop of precious liquid.

Then he walked back up the path, kicking at the railway sleepers with the toes of his trainers. They were not sleepers at all, they were not even made of wood, they were precast concrete paving blocks, grained and chipped, made to look used and weathered. There were specially designed holes through the ends where the rails had supposedly been secured by spikes.

On the edge of the lawn he stopped and called to Sandy, 'What do you think?'

She looked at the lanterns with him. 'Spooky.' A twist in her tone, a hint of mimicry, to signal that she was using the word of the moment.

He had expected the effect to be merely amusing in a self-consciously kitsch way, a jokey African Halloween no scarier than a gutted pumpkin. But the mask-heads, streaming light from their eyes, mouths and noses, were chilling. It confirmed one of Ruth's half-serious propositions about *Curiouser*: that he had chanced upon a talent for frightening people, for giving them goosebumps by doing violence to their ordinary clutter.

'I think I'll put a couple in the shrubbery.'

He went towards the house, waggling his fingers creepily.

'These things are disgusting.' Rubbing at the table-top again. 'The birds have shat all over them.'

'Weavers.'

'Do you have to clean them every time you use them? What a drag.'

'Nothing we can do about it.'

'Scare them off. Take a few potshots with your famous Luger. A bit of gunplay.'

He made a dismissive gesture with his hand and went inside. As soon as he was out of sight, she knelt at the edge of the pool and rinsed her rag in the water.

Gunplay. He had indulged in some of that, for effect.

Once – this was before Ruth's time – he had locked himself out of his house. He was living in Bellevue then and drinking too much. He could have called a locksmith, but instead he had fetched a pistol from his car and tried to shoot out the lock like a desperado. Rather than springing apart as it was meant to, the stupid thing jammed, and he needed the Lock Wizard after all.

Then there was his William Tell act with the garden gnome, when one of the bullets ricocheted and passed straight through the lounge (people said) where Ruth was watching television. In truth, she was not even home that afternoon. This particular bullet was never found. There was the hole in the blind and, using some rudimentary ballistics picked up in *Homicide: Life on the Stree*t, it was easy enough to figure out where the hole in the opposite wall should be. But it wasn't there.

Such stories got around. The cynics said that was the point: he would do anything to attract attention.

And then there was *Bullet-in*, a photographic sequence inspired by Huambo, the most battle-ravaged place he had ever seen. The buildings were so full of bullet holes it was laughable, like the set of a Clint Eastwood movie. On a pockmarked wall he found a fragment of untouched plaster in the shape of a man, as if someone had been shot there and left behind a stencil of his body. This first image was the only one made by chance: those that followed were produced deliberately, with live rounds and a template, in the trouble spots of the world. According to the official account, anyway, the one you read in the catalogue. Unofficially, they had all been made here in Greenside without a shot being fired – he was too afraid of hurting someone, and Ruth would never have allowed it. He drilled the holes in his own garden wall with a Black & Decker, and repainted the surface between photographs, patching the cracks with Polyfilla, putting together Latin American colour schemes, tatters of Middle Eastern advertising, scraps of graffiti. Waiting for the weather to turn.

His personal favourite supposedly came from the hills of KwaZulu-Natal. It showed three angular figures, a segment of a human chain, outlined in bullet holes against a mud wall. Modelled on the Guronsan C tube.

When he was finished with the series, he replastered the wall for the last time and painted it white again. In daylight you could make out the brighter patch. On an impulse, he put the last of his lanterns at the foot of this wall as a private marker. Then he went to take a shower before the guests arrived.

Bullet-in. He had arrived at this after a little improvisation. Bullet*in*, Bullet(in), Bullet•in. It was compulsive. Take the last show: CurioUSER, CURIOuser, [Curio]user, Curio_user, Curio>>>user. He had been through countless variations, riddled with characters from the little-used ranges of the keyboard. In the end: *Curiouser*. Plain and simple. Part of the new restraint which he intended to make his hallmark.

The new restraint. Where should one draw the line? The world was so loud, and no one took seriously a thing that didn't attract attention to itself. There was no room for subtlety. Things were either visible or not, their qualities were either shouting from the surface or silent. This silence, the lull behind the noisy surface of objects, was difficult and dangerous. You never knew what it held, if anything. How were you to judge whether the voice you heard was a deeper meaning, whispering its secrets, or merely the distorted echo of your own babble?

The lanterns cast an unexpected shadow over the company. Usually their friends needed little help to be rowdy. A couple of bottles of Blaauwklippen's Sociable White – the affordable plonk for sociable whites, as he said to Ruth – and they could be relied upon to misbehave. But tonight the mood was sombre and guarded. People were talking quietly in little groups, hunched against the night, as if they were afraid of being eavesdropped upon by these glowing heads with candlelight spilling around in them like drunken thoughts. It made Ruth anxious. She kept trying to communicate this anxiety to him, turning her head aside and widening her eyes in exaggerated alarm.

'Can I top you up?' Simeon leaned over the table between Leon and his new girlfriend. They were hearing about Uganda from John and Philippa.

'I'm hungry,' said Leon.

'My assistant has lit the fire.' Simeon filled their glasses.

My assistant. Despite the mocking emphasis, he liked the phrase. It gave him the same soft-shoed kick he'd got earlier when Sandy mentioned *the office*. He was turning into a little business. It irritated the hell out of Leon. He wanted to be a little business too, he wanted a manager and a personal assistant – stuff that, he wanted to be *an industry* – but he was just another muddler.

'We've been talking about *Curiouser*,' Philippa said.

'Don't let me stop you. Go on, tell me the good bits.'

'You know what's amazing? It's like you're deconstructing the whole curio thing, which seems pretty obvious. But then you're saying, yelling actually: Look, I'm deconstructing this curio! So then it's like you're deconstructing the deconstruction thing, know what I mean? That's really amazing.'

'I think it's more about *re*construction,' said John. 'It's about putting things together in new ways.'

'And how are you going to put something together again if you haven't taken it apart? That's what's amazing. I'm like, what is this thing? I'm looking at it and thinking: What am I looking at? What is it? Bits and pieces of elephant. Kudu salad. The do-it-yourself zebra. Know what I mean?'

'I liked the rhino,' said James, drifting closer, 'the skinny rhino. Norman Fischhoff bought it.'

'Oh really?' said Leon.

'The rickety rhino.'

'I'm not surprised,' said Philippa. 'It's beautiful.'

'In a sly way, I suppose,' said John. 'You don't have to be an art historian to see it's poking fun at Hirst's pickles. Those lab specimens are designed for the squeamish, aren't they? Your rhino's kind of clean-cut and cute, the way it fits together, snug as a puzzle. That pink on the cross sections is wonderful.'

'Wood primer.'

'I thought it was natural.'

'Pink wood primer.'

'Love that colour.'

'My best is the crazy paving,' said Philippa. 'Amazing.'

'"Baloney."'

'Why "Baloney"?'

'Jesus, you're slow on the uptake.'

'That's the colour!' said John. 'Polony, Escort French Polony.'

'I hear you've got some more of these doodads,' Leon said.

'Couple of hundred. Mainly masks.'

'Hundreds?' Everyone laughed. 'Well, we know what you'll be doing for the next five years. *Curiouser II*, *Curiouser III*…'

'Consider yourself lucky. You won't have to look at my work again until, let's see, 2010.'

Leon's girlfriend – Simeon had forgotten her name – said, 'Where did you get them?'

'I've heard this saga already,' said James, receding swiftly, as if his moorings had been cut. 'Think I'll move to the better wine.'

'Tell us,' said Leon, 'I want to hear.'

'Well, I got more than I bargained for, I can tell you that. I was just looking for a few knick-knacks to use on a set-dressing job. Bra Zama's African Eatery.'

'I hear the food's amazing.'

'You remember I did the décor? With Gemma at the Frame Up? It turned out to be tricky finding masks, of all things. These guys are very protective of their turf. It's a whole big secret international network, passing mainly through back doors and legal loopholes. Then I met this guy at Bruma, one of the curio-sellers, name of Roger. A Malawian. He said he thought we could come to an arrangement. He asked some connection at the next stall to watch his goods and hustled me into the shopping centre, to that Toasted Bagel place, for coffee.

'"I've got what you're looking for, but it's difficult." How so? "The goods belong to my friend Victor." Does he want to sell? "Oh yes." Perhaps we can go and see him together? "Impossible." You could ask him to call me. Does he have a cell? "I don't think so…he's been dead for six weeks."'

Laughter, loud enough to turn heads. Simeon had told this story before and was getting better at it. It helped that everyone was a little tipsy. You could always count on the Sociable White.

What had become of poor Victor? Apparently he'd been shot dead on the pavement outside a block of flats in Berea. 'The Metropolitan? You know the one?' Roger had asked. But

Simeon did not want the details, thank you very much. The day before he died, Victor had received a large shipment of masks, as it happened, and they were gathering dust in a factory in Doornfontein. Roger was planning to take over the order himself, but he would be just as happy, happier in fact, to get rid of them all at once. There was a widow back home in Lilongwe with children to feed, and a lump sum would come in useful.

The next Saturday, Simeon picked the Malawian up on a corner in Berea and drove him to Doornfontein, looking over his shoulder all the time. One read these stories about Nigerian con men practising routines so standard they had names and numbers, the 'Black Money' swindle, the 419 scam. They parked the car in End Street and went into a shabby four-storey building, walked up the widest staircase Simeon had ever seen, the risers faced with metal. What had they been manufacturing up here? The space beneath the corrugated-iron roof was cold and empty. There were windows down one wall, and, huddled together in a corner as if for warmth, five or six machines whose purpose he could not fathom, although a defunct terminology rolled through his mind – presses, lathes, gins, jennies. An abandoned sweatshop, smelling of damp cement and engine oil.

The goods were at the back behind a locked, metal-plated

door: half a dozen slatted wooden crates with the shipping details pasted to their sides. Roger jemmied one open, tossed out a few handfuls of shredded paper, and held up a mask, a moonface carved in dark wood, with slitty eyes and a toothless mouth, good-natured and foolish. Something stirred in Simeon's head, in that corner of it where his work began. He made a show of examining the mask, inside and out, with a connoisseur's eye, and ran a critical fingertip over a hairline crack, while Roger scooped out more of the paper and stacked another four or five on the floor. He did not know exactly how many items there were in each crate and had no wish to unpack them to make a count. Take it or leave it.

While Simeon was speaking some others had drifted closer, Marge, Lorraine and Bheki, all of them sceptical and intent. His story faltered.

'To cut a long story short,' he said, 'I had to have them, I couldn't resist. I made him an offer.'

Silence for a moment, while the obvious rejoinder echoed in several minds. Then Leon: 'How much?'

'A couple of grand.'

'For the lot?'

'Per crate.'

'How many in a crate?'

'It varies.'

'Do you know what these things are fetching on the street?'

'Eighty bucks, a hundred bucks.'

'And that doesn't tell you something?'

'Should it?'

'Please. This whole sob story about Victor and his widow. The stuff's obviously fallen off the back of a truck.'

'I suppose it might have.'

'You're dealing in stolen property, you shit.'

'I'm hardly *dealing*. Mind you, it's quite a nice twist. If you consider how much African art has been swiped by the real dealers, the wheeler-dealers.'

'I'm sorry, you'll have to explain. How is this different?'

'I'm an African, for one thing.'

'You mean you're black.'

'That's not what I said.'

'This Roger,' James butted in, 'the seller, the fence – he was an African too.'

'I'll bet he wasn't a bloody Malawian though,' said Leon.

'The whole business is probably a front.'

'For what? Sock puppets?'

'Sim!' Sandy called from the house. 'Simeon! Phone for you.'

Simeon went inside. He put on the pad again, became aware of it, stretching his stride, felt the elastic in tendon and sinew, toned it down a bit, sleeked back his risen hackles, before he gave the game away. More and more, he wanted to attach value to disconnected, insignificant moments like these. This was how he should express himself, he decided. In entirely private performances, meant for his own eyes only. Not even that: for his own mind's eye. This was art, everything else was advertising.

He half expected when he got inside to find that Sandy had made up an excuse to call him away. She could always smell a fight brewing, and Leon was so easy to rile, any nonsense would get him going. Ruth had been widening her eyes at him too behind Leon's back, *flaring* her eyes: for God's sake, don't start. But there really was someone on the line. Tanya, to say she couldn't make it, she'd been held up.

At gunpoint?

No really, Simeon, unavoidably detained.

Know how it is. Terribly sorry. We'll talk.

After he put the phone down, he sat in the darkened room with his hand resting limply on the receiver in its cradle.

He leaned forward to look out of the window. Nearly everyone was still gathered around the table in the garden, one big happy family, talking and laughing. Ruth would be pleased. She so badly needed the people she knew to be together in this close-knit way. John and Philippa had gone to examine the lantern against the *Bullet-in* wall. John called out to the others, some crack about how Keith Kirsten, the nurseryman, could make a fortune out of these, and people laughed. Leon had taken over the braai, just as Sandy said he would. Good for him. Good for her.

Simeon leaned back again, lit a cigarette, and thought about Tanya's call. It was irritating that she wouldn't be coming. Possibly insulting. *Curiouser* had been a success, she owed it to him to show her face.

Could the masks have been stolen? It hadn't occurred to him before, but now that the idea had been put into his head it seemed more than likely. What did a Malawian look like? There had been a Malawian kid at school with him, a couple of classes below, the son of a diplomat – 'from a diplomatic family,' his mother said. Was Freddie Chavula typical? He could hardly remember now what he looked like. The only other Malawian he could picture was Hastings Banda. The President-for-Life had acquired an African first name in his old age, but the colonial label stuck. Hastings. Christ.

Roger – the fence, as James had called him – did not do deliveries. Simeon had to organize a van himself, James's bakkie, and then they had to make two trips. The bakkie was such a clapped-out old thing, and the crates were bigger than he'd remembered. Even with Roger helping, he'd just about put his back out. When they got to Greenside, he had to rope in a couple of street guards to offload the crates into the garage. He got them to carry the one Roger had already opened straight into his studio. It was just as well Ruth was out.

The idea for *Curiouser* must have been in his mind from the start. He recalled the elemental excitement that churned through his body, something like water in dry channels, a disquieting anticipation that was almost painful, when he began to unpack his purchase, when mask after mask issued from that first crate, along with handfuls of crumpled paper covered in French, and African languages that were not at all familiar. The apparent endlessness of the supply was amusing and compelling. A shadow of the potential art work was already forming under the influence of this excess. Excess.

He splashed the concept around in his mind. Wasn't it one of the keys to understanding contemporary style? If you had one of anything, it was simply an object; if you had three, it was a design; if you had three hundred, it was a work of art. On a large enough scale, with sufficient repetition, everything became conceptual, whether you were talking about art or murder.

He'd unpacked the second and third crates in a fever, piling the masks on the floor of his studio, amassing them. He wanted to see them heaped together. He wished his hands were large enough to scoop them up like grain, to let them trickle through his fingers. He needed to feel this excess, this accumulation, to measure it with his own body.

The fourth crate brought him to an abrupt halt. It was full of animals, an African menagerie carved in wood. He packed them out on his trestle tables, like Noah releasing his charges into a new world: herds of impala, springbuck and giraffe, flocks of wading birds, the Big Five in a reserve of their own behind the computer.

The décor at Bra Zama's could not wait: he had to put aside the animals and go back to the masks. He picked out a few dozen of the finest and stored the rest in his study, which was hardly ever used. The chosen ones were arranged in little families and teams. Then he set about them with saws and drills, roughing them up, scarifying them, shearing off the tips of noses and ears, lopping and gouging. It was, Gemma said of the results, like something you would see on *Special Assignment* when Jacques Pauw, a television newsman with the manners of an undertaker, made one of his ghoulish safaris north of the border looking for witnesses to an atrocity or survivors of a massacre.

In the month or two he devoted to the Eatery, the animals stood around in his studio. From time to time he herded them into new configurations. And he spent an afternoon photographing them in the garden, setting the buck out to browse on a savannah of unmown kikuyu and the leopards to lurk in jungles of lily and fern.

Yet when he turned his attention to them properly, he found himself cutting them into pieces. Perhaps it was the smell of sawdust in the air from the savaged masks that set him off, and the proximity of saws. One day, as if the impulse had come from nowhere, he took up a tenon saw and with a sort of professional curiosity, as if the whole thing were simply a practical exercise, sliced an impala in half. It was telling, given how many creatures there were to choose from, that he took one from the bottom of the food chain. He wanted to see what it looked like inside, what it consisted of under the varnish. He watched the white sawdust sifting down onto his fingers. He turned the lopped hindquarters over and examined the pale, grainy wood that was its raw material.

Sawing, sawn. Already his arm was itching to do it again, to cut down through solid substance, and keep cutting down through it until his muscles ached.

So a single gesture had grown into the primary dynamic of his work, replicated a thousand times. It was always easy afterwards to find the motives and themes, to sniff out the references to this art work and that style, but at the time it felt to him like nothing but a mechanical compulsion, a tirelessly repeated dismemberment.

The first small pieces were simply animal figures sawn into chunks and displayed like butcher's carcases on marble chopping boards. Then came a series of rhinos and elephants sliced into cross sections a centimetre thick, vertically or horizontally, and reassembled with variable spaces between the sections, so that certain parts of their bodies were unnaturally elongated or thickened. They were like distorted reflections in a hall of mirrors. Later, after he'd acquired the bandsaw which allowed for thinner cross sections and more precise cuts, he could graft the parts of different animals into new species, the head of a lion, the horns of a buffalo, the legs of a hippopotamus, exquisite corpses, many-headed monsters for a contemporary bestiary. The pieces were presented in glass display cases with mock scientific seriousness, as if they were taxidermic specimens. The effects were uncanny – 'spooky' was the description he came to – the studio turned into a museum of unnatural history.

When he tired of tinkering at new creatures, he set himself another challenge: how far could a single curio be made to go? How thin could you slice it? In his three 'Baloney' sculptures (springbuck, impala, kudu) the cross sections were spread out flat like pieces from a puzzle, in sequence from horn to hoof. They were beautiful, everyone said so. Abstract images that were constantly jittering off the surface, straining towards a figurative existence in three dimensions.

'Crazy Paving', the centrepiece of the *Curiouser* show, was laid out on the gallery floor. It contained cross sections of twenty different species and covered a surface of nearly fifty square metres. It looked like an aerial photograph of a newly discovered planet.

An unopened crate still stood in the garage. Ruth and Sandy had pestered Simeon to open it, but he treasured it instead, somewhat superstitiously, as an investment in the future. A risky one. What if it was full of wooden spoons or soapstone ashtrays?

⎯⎯⎯

Through the window he saw Amy – her name came back to him now – walking towards the house, and in a few moments he heard the bathroom door shut.

Leon at the braai, turning the coils of wors over expertly with the tongs, careful not to break the skin. He took such fussy pride in his masculine accomplishments – fly-fishing, reverse parking, making a potjie, pitching a tent. He was a walking catalogue of stereotypical male behaviour. Wearing a string vest in the middle of winter like a teenager just to show off his tattooed arms. Drinking out of the bottle. He was like a character in a Tom Waits song, an accountant passing himself off as a sailor on shore leave. When he was younger, his accomplishments had extended to brawling over women and art, and gestures full of ferocious temper, overturning tables, slapping people, dashing drinks in their faces, acts that made the aggressor look more ridiculous than the victim. Once he had smashed a window, cutting his knuckles in the process, to get at some imagined rival, and then received such a thrashing he could not pick up a brush for a month. In the end, all that came of the whole drama was his 'Self-Portrait with Black Eye'.

People said they were two of a kind, Simeon and Leon, angry youngish men, but Simeon knew that Leon was the original and he himself the copy. His own riotous behaviour, the fist fights and gunplay, the reckless moves with chainsaws and jackhammers, had been an imitation of Leon's style. But he had never been able to carry it off. He lacked something, he lacked passion. Another Oprah quality. He had tried to cultivate it for a while, but when he became a man he put it aside and set about the pursuit of grace, to which he thought himself more naturally inclined.

Of course, Leon was also calmer now. Perhaps they were simply growing older. These days his jealousies stretched no further than a desperate resentment. Where once he might have rushed in, now he would storm out. You could hear him kicking the fender of his own car in the street, careful not to hurt his foot.

The toilet flushed, the door opened and shut, but Amy did not pass the window where Simeon sat waiting, drumming his nails on the telephone table. Was she putting something up her nose?

Simeon found her in the study looking off-balance and uncertain, facing the wall layered with masks as if she had stage fright. The sheer profusion was disconcerting, he knew, like a pavement display standing up on end. It made you feel that the room had toppled over on its side.

'Interesting installation.'

'Actually it's just a storeroom.' She looked hurt and he quickly went on, 'I mean they were cluttering up my studio, and I could hardly work with them watching me, so I hung them up here to get them out of the way. But I can see it developing.'

'There's something frightening about it. It's like a crowd, isn't it?'

'Yes.' Exactly the effect he'd been after at Bra Zama's. 'Or a mass grave. Cassinga.'

She stepped backwards until she bumped against the opposite wall, spread her arms out and pressed her palms flat.

'Is that how it works then, when you make art? Things just develop.'

'Sometimes. I'll be looking for a place to put things, you know, to get rid of them in a way. And it turns into a work. Things do shape themselves if you give them the space, they find a way of hanging together.'

'If you give them enough rope?'

They both laughed. She stepped away from the wall and passed slowly in front of his desk, looking down at his papers, spun a page around with her forefinger so that she could read it, browsing, but so frankly he could not be offended.

'I liked *Curiouser*.'

'*Curio-user*.'

'Not *Curiouser*? As in Alice.'

'No, *Curio-user*. As in a user of curios.'

This was a game he played. Whatever pronunciation someone chose, he corrected them to its opposite.

'I thought of *Curio-user*, actually. It's less obvious and somehow also pretentious. Knowing you, I went with the obvious.'

'What on earth do you mean?'

'The obvious, what's there, staring you in the face, might finally be more interesting than what's behind things. If anything.'

'Did I say that?'

'Well, that's what I understood you to be saying in that interview you did with Jackie Wetzler.'

'God, I didn't think anyone actually read those things. I thought I could say what I liked.'

'You didn't mean it then?'

'I was pulling her leg, I'm sure.'

There was a mask on the desk, being put to use as a paperweight, and she leaned over it, gazing down as if it were her reflection in the varnished surface.

'So you're going to go on with these things. Carving them up and so on.'

'Yes, I expect so.'

'Why not just leave them here. Put a sign on the door: *Curiouser and Curiouser.*'

'That's good.'

'It's quite beautiful just as it is, before you've done anything to it.'

She allowed her head to sink between her shoulders and tilted her face. Her hands were cupped on either side of the mask and it looked as if she was going to stoop and kiss its rough-hewn lips.

'They're all the same,' he said. 'Mass-produced. Made in a sweatshop like soccer balls or running shoes.'

'The expressions are different.'

'These two are the same.'

He unhooked a mask from the wall and placed it beside the

other on the desktop. He stood next to her, with his hand close to hers, closer than was strictly necessary, looking down at two round mouths and four heavy-lidded eyes.

'They're not really the same,' she said, 'if you look at them properly. They're like brothers. There's a family resemblance.'

'Granted, they're not identical. But let's say the differences are unimportant.'

'They might have been made by the same person.'

'Not necessarily.'

'I'll bet the people who made these things can tell them apart. They would come in here and pick their own work off the walls just like that.'

She clicked her fingers, three small firecracker explosions. Then she dropped her hand onto the mask and ran the tip of her middle finger along the ridged surface of its lips. In this tender gesture a human being became visible, a man with a chisel and a mallet.

Simeon turned away and perched on the edge of the desk, gazing at the mass of masks. By invoking the makers, the hands and eyes behind these things, she was changing them subtly, and it irritated him. He had become used to thinking of them as a single element, as raw material, and it suited him.

He glanced at her profile. He should run his finger along

the living flesh of her cheek, the way she was running hers over this dead wood. He leaned closer to her. There was a tattoo on her shoulder, some sort of symbol, a thorny, impatient little hook in her flesh like a Hebrew character. He should touch it. Wasn't that its purpose, to invite a touch? Not a talking point but a touching point, a point of contact. Perhaps it matched Leon's. His and hers. He should provoke Leon for old time's sake, he should invite one of his legendary rages.

'I wonder what they would make of you. The artists.'

'Craftsmen.'

'Craftsmen then. Seeing their things sawn into pieces and reassembled as monsters. Do you think it would upset them?'

He had an uneasy inkling of where the conversation was going. He said, 'Perhaps they would see the funny side of it.'

'Probably.'

'It must be all the same to them. Salad bowls, chessmen, masks' – the unopened crate came into his mind – 'so long as they get paid for the things, I should think they don't care much what happens to them.'

'I wouldn't be so sure. I think they would care very much about the prices you're getting. It's unfair, isn't it? You carve up a cheap curio and put it in a gallery, and suddenly it's worth a packet.'

Here we go again, he thought, surprised that he had misjudged her: the contemporary art as quackery discussion. Or will it be the popular art versus high art one? How many times must I have this conversation? Is this the price I pay for being an artist? For living in a cultural backwater? And then it struck him: she was with Leon. Perhaps he'd misread her point entirely. Was it Leon's cadences he heard, Leon's colours he saw, the dark ground of the affronted painter shining up through the thin wash of her own thought?

He said wearily, 'The curio is in one system and the art work in another. If you move an object from one system into another, by the sweat of your brow, you change its purpose and therefore its value. There's no point in comparing the systems unless you want to understand this transmutation.'

'We seem to have read the same books,' she said, swivelling away towards the open end of the room. 'I'm not trying to make a big political point.'

'No?'

'I already told you I liked the show. I'd buy one of those "Baloney" things if I could afford to, I've got just the wall for it. But I can't help being aware of the balance of power, the imbalance, one should say. The way you live here, the way the people who made these masks must live.'

'And you, poor thing, sleeping on a bench at the station.'

'Oh, I'm talking about myself too, you mustn't take it personally. It's just a question of awareness, of being conscious and *staying* conscious of how things are, even if you can't change them. Especially then.'

⁓

When she had gone, Simeon fetched a beer from the fridge. He could hear laughter from the garden, but he didn't feel like being there. John and Philippa would have found their way back to Uganda, Lorraine would be hastening the decline of the inner city. He knew their topics by heart.

He returned to the study, flopped down in the chair and put his feet up on the desk. He drank from the bottle and looked at the wall.

University days. He was in the first year of a BA, young, ignorant about everything. Some Marxist firebrand whom he'd met in a Sociology tutorial, a young man with a patriarch's beard so luxuriant it looked false, had collared him in the canteen and tried to teach him a lesson about the means of production. It was shocking, he'd said, that a black kid was so out of touch. He'd put a tin of Coca-Cola down on the table between them and made him think about where it came from.

He had to think about the workers who mined the ore and manned the smelters, he had to think about the workers in the plants where the paint was made, that distinctive Coca-Cola red, and the labourers in the cane fields harvesting the sugar, and the stevedores, truck drivers and supermarket packers moving the goods to the point of sale. He even had to think about the workers who made the secret ingredient without realizing it, because the recipe was locked in a vault somewhere and known to just two living people, and these poor dupes seemed to him the most downtrodden of all.

When the lesson was over and the boy with the beard had gone off to a lecture, Simeon still sat there, looking at the plate on the table-top, at the potato chips and the congealed tomato sauce, the knives and forks, the salt and pepper sachets, the linoleum, the bricks, the corrugated iron. These things had been put here by thousands of people, tens of thousands of people, bound together in a massively complex web of work, whose most surprising characteristic was that nearly all of it was invisible and unacknowledged. He heard a noise outside, beyond the glass, the hubbub of a crowd drawing near, the people who were behind everything he touched and tasted and saw, the man-made world. They were angry, these people, the proletariat, and who could blame them, they were the angry workers rising up and advancing while he sat still, looking at his hand sticking out of the cuff of his cotton sweater, the watch on his wrist, and his fingers curled around the shiny red tin.

Simeon uncrossed his ankles on the edge of the desk, flexed his feet in the trainers, and put them down firmly on the floor. How strange that such an obvious perspective – one could hardly call it an insight – had struck him with the force of revelation.

Where had Leon picked up this girl Amy? He knew the type. They drove to their televised protests in their snappy little cars, they took their djembe drums on board as hand luggage, they gazed upon exploitation and oppression through their Police sunglasses. And all along they demonstrated that there was nothing to be done. Their radicalism consisted in making manifest the impossibility of change.

He went outside.

'Mine host!' You'd think Leon had just beaten him at arm-wrestling. 'Come and eat before the hungry masses descend and scoff it all!'

They had finished eating. Leon was picking at his teeth with the end of a sosatie skewer. He spat a piece of gristle into the dark and said, 'So, did you sell anything?'

'A couple of pieces.'

'Norman Fischhoff bought the rhino,' said James.

Why is he even asking? Simeon wondered. He's been at the gallery, he must have seen the works that were reserved. It's just a game.

'Tell them about Stockholm,' said Sandy.

'What's that?'

'I've been invited to show some pieces in Stockholm at the Kulturhuset. A group show.'

'Who's curating it?'

'Johanna Dahlberg.'

'The one who did the South African show a couple of years ago?' Leon said. 'The so-called overview.'

'That's right.'

'Well that explains it then.'

'Explains what?'

'Nothing. Let it go.'

'What?'

'The connection.'

'What is it, Leon? Come on, spit it out.'

'The invitation.'

'She's invited me because I'm black?'

'No, Sims, it's because you're an African.'

'Look! Look!' Ruth yelling from the far side of the pool.

One of the lanterns had burst into flames and was blazing like a beacon in the shrubbery. It provoked a mood of awed hilarity that lasted for half an hour, as long as it took for the lantern to collapse in a smouldering heap.

⁓

'Si!' Philippa called from the lounge. 'This one's for you!'

They were washing dishes. He dried his hands on a dishcloth, kissed Ruth on the back of her head and went to stand in the doorway of the lounge. Just the diehards left, watching TV. John and Philippa sprawled on the couch, Sandy stretched out on the carpet with her head on the pouffe, sending up smoke signals. Some guy who wrote for *Beeld* – he'd come with Marge apparently, but she'd left without him – dozing in the recliner.

He looked at the screen over their heads.

Soldiers on a bridge, beating an unarmed man. The war in the Congo, he thought, but he couldn't be sure. How could his outrage have blotted out the facts? He'd seen the footage half a dozen times: someone in the SABC newsroom was obsessed with it. Especially the scene where the soldiers throw the man, the rebel, over the railings. Or is the victim a soldier, are the perpetrators the rebels? Here it comes now. They took him by his arms and legs, and swung him backwards and forwards, building up momentum, building up suspense, like children threatening to throw someone into a swimming pool, will we, won't we, and then they heaved him over. The camera rushed to follow him down, arms and legs flailing, missed most of his plummet, but caught the splash as he hit the water below. A moment of relief – he's landed in the water, he's survived! – as he scrambled to the bank. But then the soldiers – the rebels? – leaned over the railings to shoot at him, dashing from one side of the bridge to the other for the best vantage point, firing with casual gestures, taking potshots, like children playing at war, as if the sound of gunfire came from the corners of their mouths rather than the rifles in their hands.

A wick of rage sputtered in the back of Simeon's mind. He saw how this evening might end. He could fetch the pistol from the Moroccan tea caddy on his bedside table, where it lay in a jumble of spare keys and foreign currency, the small change brought back from his trips and kept for luck, an expired passport, a rubber key ring shaped like the figure in Munch's *Scream* which had been given to him by Johanna Dahlberg.

He could lurch out into the garden and stumble along beside the pool with the pistol dangling from his hand. 'S. Majara.' The hero of his own drama. Putting the unsteadiness on a bit, pretending to be drunker than he is, behaving wildly, just for himself. Four of the lanterns are still burning. He aims at the one next to the street door, because it's furthest away, and fires. A face topples into the lounge window, a terrified face looking blindly out: the man from *Beeld*, awakened from his slumber, yet again, by distant gunshots. Sandy hustles him away from the window and someone puts out the light. Sandy or Ruth or Philippa will make sure the reporter keeps his trap shut – it is still illegal to discharge a firearm in a built-up area – but the story will get around anyway. Life in the old dog yet. Tanya will be furious that she missed the fun and games.

Crime Scene. A charred mask. Perhaps one of those that burst into flames earlier will be usable. If not, he can blacken it up with a blowtorch. What was the word Sandy used? *Gunplay*. A synthesis of *Bullet-in* and *Curiouser*. 'Crime Scene I': a charred mask, gouged and gaping, made to gape more chillingly. The wound is in the forehead, an exit wound, drilled with the Black & Decker. The pale wood chipped away around the hole is white as bone.

'Crime Scene II': another mask, more severely scorched, with bullet holes in the left temple and the jaw. Protruding from the wounds, to mark the trajectories of the shots, two long wooden dowels in luminous colours. Something he saw on *Homicide: Life on the Street*.

'Crime Scene III': the real loser. Burnt beyond recognition but gleaming white everywhere, as if the fire has pared the wood down to a skull. This victim has a little flag fluttering from his broken crown.

A room full of death masks, dangling from the ceiling on fishing line – the average man is 1.75 metres, the average woman 1.63 – so that the height alone invites you to press your face into the smoky hollow. The eyes are shaped like keyholes and television screens.

On the screen, black men in pale suits are getting out of limousines, passing through revolving doors, crossing lobbies, harried by reporters and cameramen, walking backwards, thrusting their notepads and furry microphones into the frame, as if the tools of the trade are the real subject of the news. The peacemakers, the negotiators, the mediators. Whenever they face the cameras, their bodyguards, tall men with short blond hair and dark glasses, the only white people you see, appear in the background, looking alertly over their shoulders, gazing into the invisible corners where danger always lurks, off-screen, cloaked in the everyday.

Philippa stirred on the couch. She had slipped her hand into John's pocket and the sharp outlines of her knuckles pressed against the cloth. The man from *Beeld* shifted in the recliner and sighed.

Simeon went down the passage. He took a pack of cigarettes from his bedside drawer – the pistol had slipped from his mind, the visitors' book lying on his pillow did not enter it – and went to his studio, passing quietly behind Ruth, who was still at the kitchen sink with her hands in the suds. The smells in the studio were comforting. Damp plaster, sawdust, creosote, glue. He sat in the neon glare while the work folded from his brain, one piece out of another, sequences and series, objects and their names, stamped with Roman numerals like the descendants of a single forebear.

CROCODILE LODGE

A truck has lost its load on the R24, that's opposite Eastgate. Traffic lights are out of order on Jan Smuts Avenue at Bompas, in Roodepoort at Main Reef and Nywerheid, in Rivonia Road at 12th Street, in Sandown at Grayston Drive and Daisy.

The cadences of the traffic report were as familiar as a liturgy. Usually it was reassuring, this invocation of rises and dips and the states associated with them, a map of sensations keyed to his own body, to the ball of his foot pressing on the accelerator pedal and the palm of his hand lazing on the gear lever. It would soothe him to hear that each of the named intersections had become the hub of a failed mechanism, the end point of an incomplete trajectory, and that he was implicated in none of it, he was still on course. But this afternoon, caught in the rush hour and sensing trouble up ahead, the measured words fell on him like a judgement.

There has been an accident involving three vehicles on the N1 South before the Buccleuch interchange. Emergency vehicles –

Knew it! Must be the third time this month. How many accidents are there in Johannesburg on any given day? The radio reports capture just a fraction, those that call attention to themselves by happening in the rush hour, but there must be dozens more. How many drivers are speeding at this moment towards death or worse, towards a lifetime of walking with a stick, disabilities that will necessitate new hobbies, scars that will demand a different wardrobe? Accidents. The word hardly does justice to the symphonic play of causes. Why do people see order and purpose in the ordinary and give over the high points and low points to chance?

Someone blew past in the emergency lane. A fat bastard in a 4x4 with a name like a Japanese restaurant. There were more and more of these chancers on the road, the same set who used to favour the sleek saloon, flouting the unwritten laws of traffic. Their bulldog grilles came up in your rear-view mirror and began to nip at your wheels. Hard bodies, according to the advertising, but they looked milk-fed and soft with their puppy-fat fenders and bumpers like dodgem cars.

The unwritten laws. Say you're stuck in the slow lane, bumper to bumper, and everyone in front of you is going straight, whereas you want to turn off at the next exit. You can see the ramp ahead, an invitingly open stretch of tar. You're entitled to use the emergency lane to slip past, no question about that – but your rights have limits. There's a decent distance, a liberty you have to judge for yourself before you take it, which others won't find offensive. You can't jump the queue from a kilometre back, even if an empty off-ramp beckons, that's boorish. But once you've narrowed the distance to two hundred metres and paid some dues in wasted minutes, you can ease past and people will understand.

The vehicles involved in the pile-up at the Buccleuch interchange are on fire. Avoid that section of the N1 if you can and take an alternative route.

He saw it in the distance now, a rubbery column of smoke bulging up as profusely as if it issued from a chimney.

Someone else buffeted by on the left. When the system fails, the rules are there to be broken. He nosed out of the traffic and followed the offender along the emergency lane to the off-ramp. The freeway was useless now, might as well take the back roads through Vorna Valley and Kyalami, he'd get home sooner. Unless too many other people had the same idea… There was already a jam at the end of the ramp. You can never be sure you've made the right decision. It's like queue-hopping at the tills in the supermarket: no matter which queue you choose, the other one will be faster. Or it will appear that way to you, which amounts to the same thing. Another law.

The traffic edged towards the lights.

Vendors moved between the cars, proffering coat-hangers, rubbish bags, sock puppets, baseball caps, trays of naartjies, hands-free kits for cellphones. A balsa-wood schooner, swept up in a black boy's hands, came sailing through the Highveld air. From a distance there was an illusion of intricacy and craft; from close up it was shoddily made, stuck together with staples and glue. A slave ship, mass-produced, he supposed, by children in a sweatshop somewhere in Hong Kong or Karachi or Doornfontein. And how about this: a man with a sign around his neck – Keep South Africa Beautiful: Give Me Your Litter – holding out a waste-paper basket in one hand and cupping the other for a tip. He thought of handing something over – the cab was a mess – or rewarding him for sheer cheek with a few coins from the parking-meter stock in a compartment on the console. Thought again, as the lights changed and he jerked forward with the lane, keeping one eye on the wing mirror to make sure no one lifted anything off the back. Should have laced that cover properly, even though it was late when he dropped Josiah and the temps off in Tembisa.

Sylvia. Must let her know I'm stuck in traffic.

But his phone was not in the pocket of his jacket where he usually kept it. He rummaged through the junk on the seat beside him, paper serviettes, fliers for shocks and diffs and show days at town-house developments, sticky plastic spoons caught in the crocheted blanket that covered the vinyl. From the crack where the backrest joined the seat he raked a drinking straw, a book of matches and a Yale key. No sign of his cell. He wound up the window. The floor on the passenger side was cluttered with tools, offcuts of pine, coils of wire, half-used squares of sandpaper like little relief maps of the Namib, fast-food wrappers. He scratched the contents of the cubbyhole out on the floor. Nothing there either.

When was the last time I used the bloody thing? Took a call at the Crocodile Lodge site. No. The phone rang in my jacket pocket while I was up the ladder and I left it for the voicemail. Where was the jacket then? Hanging from a bolt somewhere on the hoarding below. Later, I called back. Firoz, at the office, wanting to know what I'd done with the VAT file. And then? Must have put it down somewhere.

He reached the end of the ramp. Three or four cars were getting across the intersection at a time. If that prick in the

Subaru would pull finger we could stretch it to five. The lights changed and he tacked himself onto the gaggle turning to cross back over the freeway. Now he meant to go straight on, homewards, but instead he found himself turning onto the N1 again, going back to the building site, going back to Crocodile Lodge to retrieve his phone, allowing the arrows on the tar to make the decision for him.

I should leave it for tomorrow, of course. It'll be dark by the time I get there; and someone's probably walked off with it anyway. But if it's lying out there ... Sylvia will be furious. She's such a worrier. Then again, she only comes in from gym at six on Wednesdays. I'll call and leave a message on the answering machine just to say I'll be late, nothing specific. Except that I don't have a phone!

He pushed into the traffic streaming towards Midrand. Twice in the space of a kilometre he thought he should call to say he'd be late, and twice he had to remind himself that the phone was gone. A broken record player, he said to himself, that's what you are.

Actually, you could not really call it gym, what Sylvia was doing these days to keep fit. It was boxing. The latest fad. When she'd started a few months back, she wanted him to join her. 'Finally, a fitness regime that'll suit you.'

'Serious?'

'It's macho stuff. Full of feints and jabs. You'll love it.'

'No, no, I get enough exercise running around on building sites. On a slow day I'm up and down a ladder fifty times.'

'And this?' Pinching a fold of skin on his midriff.

'Can't be helped. You know, men of a certain age.'

Of course, she was ribbing him because he'd been in the ring a few times when he was a kid. One of his stories, the kind you know by heart after twenty years of marriage.

His arm could not be twisted. But a month or so later, her car went in for a service and he had to pick her up at the Health and Racquet (or as he always said: the Health Racket). She was supposed to wait for him in the parking area, but he arrived early so that he could see what this 'Boxercise' was all about. It was early spring, the smell of jasmine and carbon monoxide in the air, a flare of sunset as if a huge primus stove had been left to scorch the wall of the sky. The exercise junkies were hanging out in the juice bar at the entrance like a bunch of old soaks.

He went up a flight of stairs and found a balcony with a view of the floor.

He wasn't sure what he was looking for. The papers were full of the trends – Exerboxing, Boxercise, Aeroboxing, Boxerobics. Aerobics with a bit of aggressive shadow-boxing thrown in. And something called Tae-Bo – Bo was short for Boxing – which he'd seen advertised on CNN. Looked a little more martial-artsy, full of hip swivels and hand chops. On the floor below, three different classes were in progress, but nothing that fitted this bill.

Then he saw them in a far corner where a punchbag was suspended from the rafters, three or four women, gloved up and glistening, and a couple of men too, skinny teenagers with tattoos, ranged around a black instructor built like one of the MTN gladiators. A woman in red boxer shorts rattling the speedball. The instructor (the *trainer*, they would say) put his shoulder to the heavy bag, and one of the women, a woman he now recognized as Sylvia – not so much by her features, which were hidden under a bulky headguard, but by the way she moved, a signature slide of the hips beneath the boxer's crouch and dance – squared up to the bag and let rip. She had the head-bob, the hooks and jabs, the nifty footwork, all put together with a ferocity that surprised him. My wife, the middleweight. He watched with grudging and guilty amazement as she threw everything she had at the bag, while the trainer kept it steady or let it sway, and then he sneaked out to wait in the bakkie. Didn't say a word when she came out flushed and sweaty, just looked out of the corner of his eye at her fist, clasping the handbag strap, and drove.

That very night, or it may have been a few nights later, his Wilkie Pieterse dream returned. Wilkie had done this before, stayed away for years, until it seemed he'd retired for good, then unexpectedly made a comeback.

It is a boxing dream. He and Wilkie are facing one another in the ring. An enormous ring, meant for men rather than boys, with ropes as thick as a man's arm, and Wilkie in his outsize shorts, satiny and shimmering in the powdery haze rising up from the canvas, the skirl of pipes like a white emanation in the air, the big red gloves, a clamouring bell. They circle, toe to toe, tapping and cuffing harmlessly. Then he feels his fists contracting, the two bulbs of the gloves beginning to beat like swollen hearts, his muscles acquiring iron and oil. His fists drive out from his body in a rush of steam. He turns into a boxing machine, he pummels Wilkie Pieterse mercilessly, mechanically, until blood spurts from his nose and ears and eyes, and he falls to his knees. A bell starts to ring and a man appears, pastel pale and clean as a male nurse, waving his palms to show that the bout is over, but his fists have a life of their own, they keep springing out from his body, thudding into the other boy's face, until at last the bell dissolves in the morning's alarm.

The dream had lingered for days, because this ending came as a surprise. He'd been fighting Wilkie in his sleep now for forty years, on and off, ever since his final glimpse of that little twerp in the waking world, clanking through the turnstile behind the grandstand at the Caledonian Sport and Recreation Club. Always, Wilkie beat him black and blue. This was his first victory. It left him feeling strangely dissatisfied.

***

Observe safe following distance. Always see three arrows.

He usually slowed down when he saw the sign, so that there were three painted arrows on the tar between the bonnet of his bakkie and the tail of the car in front. He was exactly the kind of person this experiment in inculcating sensible driving habits was aimed at: attentive to the rules and regulations and willing to take instruction. But in rush-hour traffic on a Wednesday afternoon there was no point even trying to comply. No sooner had a gap opened up in a lane than someone barged into it, convinced that it would get him to his destination more quickly. The experiment had the opposite of its intended effect: it triggered a reckless Pacman instinct in people that made them want to gobble up arrows and catch the car in front.

He saw two arrows, one arrow, two arrows, as the lane expanded and contracted to an unpredictable rhythm. He thought about braking distances. He had read somewhere that if you sneeze at 120 kilometres an hour, and the average sneeze lasts seven seconds, counting the bleary-eyed build-up and the snotty aftermath, effectively you're driving blind for more than two hundred metres. Could it be true? He readjusted the side mirror with the toggle on the door panel, started converting kilometres per hour into metres per second in his head, let it go, tried to remember precisely what had become of his phone.

⁓

A boxing machine? It was like something out of *Popular Mechanics*. 'Machine throws combinations, mows lawn, makes ice cubes.' Sometimes he thought the whole shape of his life was caught between those pages, preserved there as a kind of fate, like a timetable left behind in the nineteen-fifties. A bookmark.

Lying on his bed in the afternoons, with the sun beating down through the window on the backs of his legs, reading his father's magazines. There were piles of them on the shelves in the garage going back to the years after the War, tatty things that had never seen the inside of a library, at home rather among tins of grease and bottles of brake fluid, the clutter of spare parts and spanners and nuts and bolts. In the school holidays, he brought them into his room a dozen at a time, a year of monthly volumes, and they lay on his bedside table reeking of rubber and petrol, troubling his dreams with their fumes. He would go through them again and again, until he knew the images by heart.

It was an American world he entered there, its surfaces airbrushed to perfection, gleaming with old-fashioned optimism; and its inner workings laid bare, frankly and practically, as the product of enterprise and effort. This double world expressed itself in two languages: the patter of leisure and convenience, of patios and porches, rumpus rooms and dens, pool tables, lazy Susans, TV trays; and a deeper music of planning and building, of lathes and drill presses, bandsaws and welding irons, bits and gauges. He wanted to acquire these languages himself, he wanted to live in this world, passing effortlessly between its countersunk dimensions, where he felt he belonged.

In these well-thumbed pages all things were the sum of their parts. A slatted bench for the garden, a rocking horse for the nursery, a toolshed, a boathouse, an entire mansion made of wood. On the plans that accompanied the do-it-yourself projects every solid thing had been exploded, gently, into its components, arrangements of boards, springs, rails, nails, veneers, bushings, cleats, threads. Each part hovered just out of range of the others it was meant to meet, with precise narrow spaces in between. All it needed was a touch, a prod with the tip of a finger, to shift everything closer together, and a perfect whole would be realized, superficially complete and indivisible. Until then each element waited, in suspension, for finality. Not a single nut or bolt or washer had been forgotten; every last screw was poised a quarter of an inch away from the hole into which it would soon be driven, vibrating in the yellowed air of the paper, emitting what the boy, lying on his stomach with the open magazine propped against a pillow, took to be anticipatory music.

Want to be an engineer?

Yes, he thought, I want to be a popular mechanic. I want to wear these chiselled features, clench this square jaw and narrow these appraising eyes. I want crisp waves carved into my hair, as hard and smooth as scrolled maple. I want to work with an angular briar jutting from my lips like a speech bubble, a fragrant and stubborn Dr Watson. *Now you can be a crackerjack.* 'Knurled thumb nuts used throughout.'

But he had not become an engineer. He had worked instead for contractors, friends of his father, on small-scale building operations and alterations, and then for a couple of larger construction companies supervising minor procedures, clearing and levelling sites, excavating foundations, digging ditches or backfilling them. At thirty, with a family to support, he was not the success he wanted to be. He went out on his own, starting the first of many businesses, teaching himself to plant telephone poles, renovate swimming pools, fell trees – the 'Tree Feller' he called himself in that phase – losing money, losing interest.

His latest venture had been the most enduring and lucrative: putting up billboards.

Billboards are big business, he would tell anyone who asked. The outdoor advertising giants ran thousands of hoardings, including massive eight- and ten-storey structures along the freeways, bus-stop displays on suburban streets, painted walls in the city and electronic boards at the malls. He was in a different league, dealing with small boards, seldom more than thirty or forty square metres, for advertisers and property developers. Over the years he had done more and more real estate, inexpensive structures with a limited lifespan: the board announcing a new development stayed up while the construction was under way, advertising office space or town-house units for sale, and then it came down again. His connections in the building trade helped to rustle up business. There was not much competition, but then there was no ready demand either: many of the companies simply put up their own boards and needed persuading that a specialist could do a better, cheaper job of it. The sheer volume of development in the city kept him busy. As high-rises and office parks went up on smallholdings in Sandton and walled town-house complexes were set down in the veld around Midrand, the northern outskirts of the city began to regard themselves as its centre and the projects became more grandiose.

The Crocodile Lodge billboard was larger than usual and it had taken a week to put up. It was on rocky ground, on a sloping stand beside the N3, and sinking the posts had been a performance. Josiah and his team were breaking rock with a jackhammer for a solid day while the agency breathed down his neck, complaining that they couldn't put in their invoice until the whole job was done. They even insisted on pasting up the sheets themselves, a ponytailed art director with a team of workers in white overalls, all of them white too. University students, he discovered. There was a University of Advertising, apparently, and this was one of their assignments. The ponytail brought a canvas chair and an easel to hold the design, as if it were a masterpiece rather than a simple jigsaw, and under his direction the students unfurled and attached the numbered sheets. An artist's impression of the town-house complex came into view, a tidy, toy-town version of the bushveld. It was the first time he had seen a complex with an African theme, the safari lodge, all sandstone and thatch.

As Crocodile Lodge appeared, block by block, he found himself leafing again in memory through the pages of *Popular*

Mechanics. He remembered a holiday house on the cover of an issue from the mid-fifties. Except for a chimney of stone, the place was made entirely of wood, in the American style, and stood on the edge of a lake (if it ever caught fire, there would be nothing left but that chimney, like a tombstone in the ashes). There was a crazy-paving porch and a cindered drive with a Chevrolet parked in it. A slipway ran down to the water, where a Canadian canoe was moored to a jetty, and on the far shore was a stand of Douglas firs, reflected in the placid surface.

He had spent many hours gazing at this picture, trying to decipher the specific meaning of America that lay in these shapes and shades, in the gloss on a fender like a smear of butter or the rune of smoke from a chimney pot mimicking a seabird. This place, impossibly distant and unreal, filled him with painful longing, an ache for containment that was peculiarly like homesickness. To be bathed in these colours, held by this light falling benevolently on every surface, aglow with prosperity and happiness.

Some people, he thought, will find the same pangs awakened by Crocodile Lodge, which was materializing slowly, archaically, as the students glued and smoothed sheet after sheet with their long-handled brooms. Monkeying around.

Dynamic Construction had done a deal with the University of Advertising. Could there be such a thing? Like that Kentucky Fried Chicken Academy in Bez Valley, where you could major in Herbs and Spices.

He wanted to go home, but they wouldn't let him: you never know, there might be problems. The only problem he foresaw was petty theft. Already there were bricks stacked up among the felled bluegums, bits of scaffolding and heaps of building sand – or was it beach sand railed in from the coast for the waterholes? They should never have delivered the materials before the contractor had established a permanent presence on the site, it was just asking for trouble. A few things had been pilfered in the past week. They would have to get a watchman. Or a company to patrol.

While the students worked, he picked his way to the edge of the site and looked out across the veld. In the sump of the valley lay the freeway, the oily N3, like a slow black river. On the opposite slopes stood two recent townhouse developments: Villa Toscana in the east and Côte d'Azur in the west. He'd put up the billboards for Villa Toscana too, as a matter of fact, but those had been struck long ago, when the first phase of the complex was finished. The Riviera is harder to capture than

Tuscany, a contractor had told him once, not so much in the renderings as in the real world, in the buildings themselves. French textures and colours are more subtle, the styles are harder to imitate. The Highveld light cooperates more readily with Italian colour schemes and that's why Tuscany is easier to reproduce. Perhaps, he'd responded, it's because the contractors have had so much practice? There were bits of Italy, a peculiar country born and bred in the colour chart, made of swatches and samples, rising everywhere on the Reef. Stage sets on which to dramatize work and leisure.

Italy, France. In a month or two, at his back: Africa. That seemed even stranger than these European islands: a self-contained little world in the African style, surrounded by electrified fences, rising from the African veld.

—

'Radio-controlled lawnmower lets inventor loaf in shade.' 'Unique floor lamp has aquarium base improvised from gasoline-pump bowl.' 'Bathroom scale folds into wall when not in use.' 'Decorative kitchen wall-light made from spoon and bowl.' Half the magazine was taken up with descriptions of gadgets and inventions, household hints and handyman's tips, objects put to new purposes or brought into new relationships with one another, improvements, adaptations and customizations. He went from one headline to another, poring over the pictures and diagrams, absorbing the innovative emanations of seemingly ordinary things. Nothing was truly itself. 'Jar covers provide small pulleys.' 'Drawing board is easily adjusted if held by storm-sash brackets.' 'Mesh tube laid in gutters prevents clogging by leaves.' This must be the meaning of America: an endless series of improvisations on the material world. A kind of jazz.

One arrow, two arrows. Spent the morning in Rivonia speaking to a new client, showing him a portfolio, talking technical. Phone rang three times: Firoz, Lewis at Dynamic, Firoz. Early lunch in the Brazilian at Rivonia Junction. Tramezzino. The waitress insisted it was a tramezzini. Called Peter John during the espresso to confirm the rugby tickets. Picked up Josiah and four guys and took them out to Crocodile Lodge. Dynamic have decided they want illumination at night and so there are lights to install. Up and down a ladder all afternoon. Phone rang a couple of times. Called Firoz back about some

VAT invoice or other. Must have lost it after that, on site. Or put it down in the cab, maybe, where someone else picked it up. Josiah's totally reliable, so's Oupa. If it's been swiped, it'll be one of the temps. There's that new guy Josiah brought along. Alan. Not a very common black name, can't recall ever meeting one before. Perhaps it's *Olun*? Looked like a Nigerian. Could it have wound up in one of the toolboxes?

The Star Stop Egoli was coming up. On an impulse, he turned off and looked for the public telephones, spotted the four units like snail shells in a face-brick alcove near the toilets. He parked the bakkie at the kerb, went to the nearest phone, fed it with a handful of parking-meter money and dialled the number of his own cell. Leaving the receiver dangling, he went quickly back to the bakkie and walked around it. His phone was programmed to play the theme tune from *Mission Impossible*. Nothing.

When he picked up the instrument to replace it on the cradle, he was surprised to hear his own voice, muffled and distant, as if he was speaking from the boot of a car. 'Gordon Duffy... The Outdoor Edge.' He put the receiver to his ear. 'I'm not available right now, but leave your name and number and I'll get back to you asap.'

A superstitious tremor shook him. He imagined the cellphone lying somewhere in the grass at Crocodile Lodge, in a place full of red ants and dry roots, and his own voice calling from it like a small creature. Or even worse, his telephone voice, disembodied and businesslike, speaking out of some thief's pocket. This thought was suffocatingly worse, choked with lint and dottle. The smell of his own aftershave and sweat rising from the plastic handset in the hot pocket of an overall. It's an intimate object, this channel for voices – he'd never seen it that way before – pressed close to your body and your thoughts, breathed into and spoken through. A catalogue of your own connections too, the pre-programmed numbers to wife, mother, son, daughter, doctor, armed response company.

The tone sounded. The idea of leaving a message for the supposed thief flickered through his mind. 'I know who you are…' Then he pictured the phone lying on a makeshift table in a shack, among beer bottles and ashtrays. Four men sitting around, drinking and smoking. He put the phone down. At least the thief hadn't answered. It's common enough for the culprit to answer and tell you to piss off. Happened to Sylvia's brother.

Instead, he called home and left a message on the answering

machine for Sylvia to find when she came in from boxing. I've been delayed, he said, I'll be home around seven. He did not say why. She did not like him messing around on construction sites after hours, especially since Manny Pinheiro got himself shot in a hijacking at Kya Sands.

Back on the freeway, with a tin of Stoney ginger beer clasped between his knees, it occurred to him that when she found the message, she would phone his cell. Please God, no one will answer. Or I'll have the thing in my hand again by then.

Traffic lights are out of order in Bedfordview at Harper and Van Buuren, in Parktown North at Jan Smuts and Jellicoe. There are roadworks on William Nicol between Ballyclare and Peter Place. The accident at the Buccleuch interchange has been cleared, but emergency vehicles are still on the scene and traffic is moving very slowly. If you can, avoid the N1 South, that's near the junction with the N3.

My thoughts exactly.

The history of exercise – this is how his boxing story usually began – someone should write a book about it. Chances are, someone has; you name it, there's a book about it. Probably a long shelf in the library by now.

I've seen most of it, starting with Jane Fonda. Seen batons, balls and weights, elastic bands and slippery boards. Dancing, stretching, skipping, stepping and twisting. Spinning on stationary bicycles. Whenever Sylvia embarks on some new fad to keep fit and stay trim, I find an excuse to pop in at the gym and see it for myself. In the beginning, it was youthful jealousy: I needed to make sure she was really there, where she said she was. Now I just like to have an image in my head of what she's up to for an hour a day, five days a week.

But boxing? I should have left well enough alone.

It was my father's idea that I should box: now that I was going to school I had to learn to 'take care' of myself, I had to be 'useful' with my fists, it was the only language a playground bully understood. So I was enrolled in Louis Moller's Boxing Academy for Boys in the gym behind the scout hall. We were taught the basics of punching and blocking. Mainly, we were made to run around the playing fields of the high school next door, to skip and do push-ups, and take cold showers.

Just a month after joining the club, I'm in my first public bout at the Golden Gloves Tournament. It's part of the annual fête organized by the Caledonian Sport and Recreation Club. A ring has been put up on the football field in front of the main grandstand and a few spectators are sitting on the benches under the corrugated-iron roof, bemused or bored. Mostly, they're strolling among the stalls and tents on the field, taking tickets at the tombola, eating pancakes and drinking beer, turning their attention to the ring only when a cheer or a jeer goes up. Many are waiting for the long afternoon of junior bouts to wear away before the serious boxing begins under floodlights in the evening. Until then, there are other diversions: Highland dancing, skydiving – the target X in whitewash on the hockey field – police dogs jumping through fiery hoops and sniffing out stolen property. In a corner near the beer garden, a black man, a bag-snatcher, is putting on a hessian overcoat with long, thickly padded arms.

The gloves are hot and soft, and slick inside with the sweat of the last boy, who's just had his nose bloodied. They cover my fists like huge wilted red peppers. The cuffs are too wide to draw tight around my wrists and so Mr Moller wraps the laces around a few times and ties a bow. A length of blue ribbon is tucked into the band of my shorts. Then Mr Moller lifts me up into the ring.

Wilkie Pieterse is no taller than me, but his limbs look hard and wiry. A pale round head, newly shaven, with a blond tuft on the forehead. He smells of wintergreen and mealie leaves.

When we spar at Moller's, we bat one another with the gloves and it's hardly worse than being hit with a pillow. But Wilkie is not one of Moller's boys: he's learned to box in some city club, a place near the station, up a green stairway that reeks of beer and cigarettes from the snooker saloon on the floor above. The bell has hardly sounded, we've hardly touched gloves, sportingly, as we're required to do, when Wilkie Pieterse hits me square in the mouth. Everything I've learned about defending is knocked out of my head by that blow. Someone is yelling at me to keep my gloves up, but I can't see, and Wilkie is punching away on the other side of the big red barrier, knocking it back into my face. After the first panic-stricken minute, I find my balance and try to make a fight of it. But I simply cannot hit him: he's too fast. He's actually dancing, doing the light-footed shuffle you're supposed to do, and flinging out punches, lefts and rights, hooks and jabs, he's got the whole vocabulary down pat. The blows he's landing on me aren't all that painful, the gloves are so thickly padded, but by the time the bell rings at the end of the first round, I could cry from frustration and shame.

In the break, I sit on a stool in the corner while Anton de Melker, one of the club's real prospects and no relation of the famous murderess, sponges my face and gives me advice. A teenager playing the big-time trainer. My eyes wander away, through the ropes, to the men dotted about on the stands, lounging with hands behind heads, legs flung over the backs of the benches in front, laughing and chatting. There's my father, waggling his head as if to communicate a strategy.

The second round is even worse. I flail at my opponent, trying to hit him rather than simply ward him off, actually aiming at him, at a point in the air behind him, trying to punch *through* him – as Anton said – and missing again and again, while the gloves bump into my face from one surprising angle and then another. Becoming enraged, growing wilder and wilder, desperate to make a fight of it, to land one blow that hurts him, and succeeding only in making myself look more and more ridiculous. Reeling, tottering, swaying. Years later, I'll make a joke of it: and in the blue corner... Tottering.

In my dream, Wilkie Pieterse batters me into submission after heroic resistance, bloodies my nose and sends me crashing through the ropes. In fact, in the harsh, sunlit reality of a Highveld afternoon, while storm clouds gathered behind the oaks and the pipes skirled in the dressing rooms under the stand where the band was preparing for their show, I finally fell over my own feet, swinging yet another roundhouse that missed, and burst out crying.

———

Approaching the site along the old road through the plots, he saw the billboard image of Crocodile Lodge in the distance, illuminated against the mildly darkening sky. The lights he had spent the afternoon installing, four metal cowls on struts that overhung the billboard like a row of gallows, had come on automatically as the day began to drain from the air. Although he knew he should hurry on to take advantage of what light remained, he could not resist pulling over for a moment to look at the board on the horizon. It would be wonderful at night, as bright and animated as a drive-in screen; but now it was softly insistent, its colours heightened so gently you would have put the change down to some shift in your own state of mind rather than an artificial light source.

Crocodile Lodge as it was meant to be, a bulwark of robust stone rising against the sunset, a printed sky redder and hotter, more full of blood and gamy juices than the ash-grey heavens behind the screen, the fading backdrop of reality. Stone, wood and thatch. The upper apartments had little gazebos instead of conventional balconies, with conical thatched roofs supported by wooden beams that mimicked the forks and stubs of indigenous trees. In the foreground, flat-topped thorn trees and waterholes edged by rushes, where the crocodiles that had given the place its name might be supposed to lie hidden.

Once it had been customary to furnish such wishful images with a notice that said 'Artist's Impression' – even though the place was an obvious imagining, a world of watercolour and stippled ink, where the trees along the avenues looked like scraps of sponge on toothpicks, and sketchy men and women went strolling on tapering, coffee-table legs. He wondered why the convention had lapsed. Now that the fanciful images were practically indistinguishable from the photographically real, were more vividly convincing in fact than the ordinary world, disclaimers were no longer required.

He drove on, looking for the gap where the fence had been taken down. And now that he was moving again, he saw clearly how such a place would come into its own in the dusk, in the burnt-out after hours of a working day. Whoever had designed the billboard must have seen it too. Leaving their offices, agencies, studios, showrooms, chambers in Sandton and Midrand, muted interiors full of cool surfaces, blinded and air-conditioned, and taking the freeways across the newly domesticated veld, the residents of Crocodile Lodge, the account executives, human resource managers, stockbrokers, dealmakers, consultants, representatives in their high-riding 4x4s and their vacuum-packed cabriolets, their BMWs and Audis, would see ahead of them not a town house but a game lodge, and their professional weariness would yield to the pleasurable anticipation of getting inside the gates before nightfall, drawing up a bar stool made of varnished logs to a counter cross-section of ancient yellowwood on a lamplit stoep, taking a beer or a glass of single malt in hand, and gazing out into the gathering darkness, where the night creatures were stirring.

He lay on his bed with the sun on his back and the fuzz of the candlewick bedspread making his forearms itch, lost in his father's America, leafing from the full-colour world on the cover of the magazine to the monochrome plans that folded out of the spine inside, from the seamless whole to the divided parts, every element named and numbered and accorded its god-given place, taking things apart in his head, putting them together again. In time, the wholes and the parts drew closer and closer together, infected with purpose, until they pressed up against one another, sometimes, and fused.

It must have started with simple objects, he supposed, with salt cellars and push toys, but what came back to him always was the holiday house on the edge of the lake. The way its plywood panels filled up with colour, the way textured finishes – Kencork, Marlite, Novoply – goosefleshed the surface of blank paper, and metallic sheens slid over beadings and facings. Having consumed the technical drawing and its qualities, the lifelike image became manipulable.

The exploded view.

He closed his eyes and began to detach the components of the house one by one as if easing apart a delicate puzzle, finding the sketchy braille of the plans on the tips of his fingers, reading the bones concealed beneath the coloured skin. He separated board from board, stone from stone. He suspended every silvery nail and brassy screw in the familiar notches and hollows of the yellow air. When he was finished with the house, he moved on to the landscape, discerning the plans at the heart of everything, uncovering armatures and seams. Even the pines on the shore he exploded into their parts, so that each needle quivered beside a sheath in a stalk, each cone burst into separate scales, and each trunk shucked its bark like a coat. The world, disassembled as precisely as a diagram in a biology textbook, sucked in bracing breath and expanded. The universe was expanding, we were causing it to expand, by analysing it.

The knack had never left him, a surgical ability to see how things fitted together. Even now, after forty years, it sometimes came in useful when he had to resolve a mechanical problem or make a repair.

But, in truth, this skill seemed to him increasingly outmoded in the world he lived in. It was no longer clear even to the most insightful observer how things were made or how they worked. The simplest devices were full of components no one could see, processes no one could fathom.

A few months before, he had read a magazine article that speculated on the fragility of human knowledge. This was the millennial premise: what if the man-made world, along with its books and records, every repository of knowledge, were destroyed by some catastrophe, and only one hundred people could be saved as the bearers of all we know. How would we choose the survivors to seed a new civilization on the other side of the deluge? Which combination of talents and proficiencies would ensure that humankind was not hurled back into the

Dark Ages, or beyond them, into an even more brutal state of savagery? What could be saved of our high-tech world? How many people knew what went into the manufacture of a fibre-optic cable, a compact disk, a silicon chip, a printing press, a sheet of paper? How was information coded digitally? People were always bandying about the notion of the 'binary system' – but how was such a thing put to a useful purpose? How was electricity generated? How was a human being placed under anaesthetic? Where did aspirin come from? PVA? Glass? What were the most important inventions of the past ten millennia? Everyone would start with the wheel. And then? If one could arrive at a list of the ten most significant inventions, would it be sufficient to nominate one expert, representing each invention, to make the voyage into the future? Were gadgets enough? There was a bias towards technology in the entire game. The invention of writing was surely more important than the wheel – as the premise of the game itself demonstrated. One would want artists in one's ark too, and a person who could read music and play an instrument or two, a multi-instrumentalist. But would it make sense to take a pianist without a piano tuner, a piano builder, a timberman? One would want a linguist, a polyglot, to preserve as many languages as possible. But would it make sense to take a speaker of Finnish, Polish, Zulu if he or she had no one else to speak to? Noah's principle, two by two, made sense. Or one could come at it from another angle entirely, aiming to preserve those abilities and inclinations, knacks and leanings, that might allow people – the descendants of the hundred – to rediscover what had been lost. Perhaps the individual language was less important than the ability to speak, the individual technology less important than the inclination to reason, the art form less important than the need to imagine. Just when that seemed resolved, a different set of priorities presented itself. Noah again. Healthy men and women, that's what we need, a good spread of genes, and the desire and ability to procreate. How would one reconcile fecundity and experience? What sort of population would one hundred healthy, genetically diverse adults generate? What did one mean by 'genetically diverse'?

The one hundred. The chosen ones. A neat number for the calculation of percentages, for taking a census. The idea appalled him at first. How little he knew! If he were one of the lucky few, a volume in the human library, what could be learned from him? How to use a rivet gun. How to take it apart and put it back together again. How to renovate a swimming pool – but not how to chlorinate a glass of water. How to erect a billboard. How to drive a car. How to box.

Finally he'd found comfort in the idea, in the simplicities it demanded. There would have to be farmers in the group, and builders, and tailors and cooks. Neither artists nor scientists were necessary. Historians, perhaps. Priests. The catastrophe was a blessing in disguise, an opportunity to purge the social body, to cut away the fatty excess of the last few centuries and return to the bony basics. A global detox. The true image of our times: the bedridden obese. The bodies that could only be removed by smashing down walls and hauling in cranes.

A truck has broken down on the N1 South before the Hans Strijdom off-ramp. That's in the right-hand lane. Traffic lights are out of order in the CBD at Market and Simmonds, at Market and Harrison, at Rissik and Bree. In Blackheath at Judges and Republic, in Florida at Beacon and Ontdekkers, in Westdene at Harmony and Perth. A car has broken down on the N3 opposite the PPC Cement Factory. A pedestrian is walking along the N12 in the Glenanda area. Please look out for a pedestrian in the emergency lane on the N12 going east.

He drew up in the sandy clearing beneath the Crocodile Lodge billboard, switched off the engine, ratcheted up the handbrake and got out. There was light in the air, but on the ground the struts of the hoarding and the lopped branches of bluegums cast a mess of long shadows. Leaning back into the cab, he switched on the headlights and flicked the lever on the steering column to bright.

Where to start? The four lights on the billboard, hanging down their heads to gaze intently at the ground, suggested that he start there. That's where they were working most of the time. But he'd walked all over the site this afternoon and the phone might be lying in a distant corner, or he might have crushed it into the earth a minute ago under the treads of his tyres.

If only I had a phone to phone my phone.

Perhaps Sylvia will call! He tilted his wrist into the beam of the headlights. Ten past six. She should be home by now. She'd come in from gym, find his message, his non-committal message, and decide to call. And he'd hear the phone ringing, *Mission Impossible*, he'd hear it piping like a field mouse in the dark somewhere and blunder after it frantically, relieved, calling out to it like a pet, and find it. What a beautiful end to the story. He actually paused, afraid that he would miss it, and cocked an ear, and held the pose a little awkwardly, for too long, felt the expectant expression hardening on his face, like an actor in a play when someone else misses a cue. Heard nothing but the distant gravel-rush of traffic on the N3, and insect noises, and a sound that was oddly congruent with these – the tick-tocking of the engine as it cooled down.

Search beneath the billboard. A grid-search of sorts. Use the pillars of the hoarding and these thick shadows to mark out territory. He went towards the pillars, and the headlights threw his shadow over Crocodile Lodge, the enormous grey blur of his head, and it reminded him of the irritating disruption of fantasy that occurs when a careless operator passes his hand in front of the lens in the projection room.

Company. He was still hunting at the foot of the hoarding when he became aware of an engine noise that was not as distant as the freeway, and a moving light, and, looking around for the source, saw a minibus coming across the plot, finding a way between heaps of sand and stone, dipping and swaying through gullies and dongas.

Run now, ask questions later. He dashed for the bakkie and slid in behind the wheel. With the ignition key between thumb and forefinger, he saw the vehicle swing round and face back in the direction it had come from, as if the driver had only just realized he'd lost his way. He hardly had time to feel relieved before reverse lights flared. The bus backed into the gap between a felled tree and a stack of bricks, where he had squeezed through earlier into this corner of the plot. They were parking him in.

Some men got out of the bus. Three of them, no, four. He heard doors bang, the rumble and thud of the sliding door at the side. The thieves who'd been filching bits and pieces off the site, no doubt. Probably after some scaffolding or a couple of bags of cement. His presence here must be an unwelcome surprise.

If I had a phone I could call for help. I could lean on the hooter. Will anyone come? Those lights there through the trees, that's a house on the other side of the old road. They probably won't hear. And even if they do, they probably won't come. These days it's every man for himself.

There was something written across the rear window of the bus, one of those blinds printed with a platitude. Something he should memorize. But he couldn't make it out in the gloom.

If I run towards the highway there's just the one fence, three strands of barbed wire, I could vault it or go underneath, leopard crawling.

He got out of the cab again. Surrender the vehicle. After

Manny Pinheiro got shot, Sylvia had done one of those courses where they taught you how to behave in a hijacking, had done it in his place, because really he was the one who needed it. She was always quoting phrases from the manual. Move slowly. Don't look them in the eye. It is not worth dying to save your car. He pushed down the lock on the door panel, lifted the handle and shut the door. Do not be a hero.

The four men were standing behind the bus. At the sound of his door closing, one of them looked across, and then away again. They were in no hurry. They were also moving slowly, not looking him in the eye. For some reason their slowness, their ease, kept him rooted. If they had rushed at him, he might have fled. Instead they were talking casually, barely acknowledging him, deliberately ignoring him, as if they were giving him time to run away. This understanding of their attitude rooted him more firmly. He shifted his weight from one foot to the other, testing the mechanics of escape like someone in a dream, trying to run away but making no progress. Running in molasses.

His movement caught their attention. Two of the men looked at him directly for the first time. A third opened the back of the bus and reached for something. The fourth walked a few paces away, unzipped his fly and began to piss. The third man shut the door of the bus with a bang. He had something in his hand, a pipe perhaps. The fourth man rezipped his pants. Now all four of them came towards him over the flattened veld grass, and then stopped again and looked around.

Where are the guns?

The cars swept past half a kilometre away.

They should have guns.

They were all the same height, all wearing the same outfit. Dark jackets, leather jackets he thought, light pants. They looked like a musical group, a quartet. Even their faces were rough equivalents of one another. Perhaps they were brothers? The members of a gang or a club? What should he memorize?

One of them was carrying the pipe he'd taken from the back of the bus. It might be a spanner for the jack. He was not pointing it or flourishing it, it was simply there, an incidental object, dangling from his fingers. He moved ahead of the others.

Walk. His knees buckled as he walked into the clearing in front of the bakkie, as if he was going to meet them, and then stopped with the headlights behind him. His body felt disjointed. He swayed, shifting his weight from one foot to the other. Molasses. Why do they always say 'molasses'?

They were wearing jackets despite the heat. The one in front, the one with the pipe, had a puffy coat, something stuffed with down. His head was round and smooth, there was a clenched look about his face, about his whole body, the hard body you had to imagine beneath the soft coat. He stopped while the others hung back and held out his hand, the hand that was not holding the pipe.

'Come. We do not want trouble.' His voice was reasonable and soft. He wanted the keys.

I should throw them into the dark like a character in a film, a small man full of bravado, standing up for himself. Let them look, let them discover how hard it is to find anything in this mess. One flick of the wrist will do it.

But instead he closed his fist, felt the key ring pressing into his palm. He was here for a reason, he saw that now, he had been given the chance to demonstrate something to these men, to himself. But what? Which qualities was he called upon to show?

His knees folded a little more, his shoulders hunched up around his ears as if his body could no longer support the weight of his head.

The man with the pipe looked curious. He said something to the others without looking back and they moved closer. What is this drunken fool up to?

They are going to beat me. He could feel their fists striking him already, knocking his face into a blur, into a buckled concertina of features, cartoonishly stupefied. I am in the light.

He saw his shadow, an enormous projection of himself, on the billboard. He was crouched over, butting the air with his fists. He was bobbing and weaving. Making patterns in the air with his head, tracing figure eights and zeds, practising a sort of calligraphy, an American art. A boxing machine. A boxing machine in molasses. A primitive thing, clankier than Gutenberg's press, driven by belts and flywheels, speaking an ancient, oily language of cranks and cams, sprockets and valves. He would resist. He would absorb the punishment and stay on his feet, a man who did not know when he was beaten. Bobbing. Weaving. Dancing.

Their disbelieving faces came closer. The one in front was holding the pipe diagonally across his body, gripping it in two places like an axe, cancelling himself out.

He saw exactly what would happen. They would beat him and hammer him and drill him. He bobbed, and ducked, and refused to fall. They struck out, as if they were driving nails into him, and with every blow he felt more like himself.

archipelago books
is a not-for-profit literary press devoted to
promoting cross-cultural exchange through innovative
classic and contemporary international literature
www.archipelagobooks.org